Prince Albert Book 3: The Realm Pirates

by Brian Daffern

Hickory Tales Publishing LLC
Bowling Green, Kentucky
2004

First Edition

Published Nov. 2004 by Hickory Tales Publishing LLC
841 Newberry St
Bowling Green, Kentucky 42103

ISBN Number: 0-9709104-7-9
Library of Congress Control Number: 2004114521

Dedication

To my loving wife. Without her continuous support and encouragement, this series would not have been possible.

Prince Albert, Book 3: The Realm Pirates

Other books available by
Hickory Tales Publishing LLC

The Promise by Charles Entwistle

BearClaw by Ron Schaaf

Quicksilver Deep by Buddy Cox

Chalmette by Charles Patton

Hoot Owl Shares the Dawn by Jennifer French

and in *this* series

Prince Albert in a Can by Brian Daffern

Prince Albert, Book Two:The Beast School
by Brian Daffern

For more information, see our website
www.hickorytales.com
or your favorite bookstore, or online bookstore site

A special thanks is given to our artist, Joyce Britton, for her imaginative cover artwork, and to her grandsons who were her inspiration.

WHAT HAS COME BEFORE

Albert, a normal boy living in a small town in California, discovers on his tenth birthday that he is the kidnapped son of an evil King from a parallel world and that his kidnappers have been pretending to be his grandparents. He instantly drifts into a coma, as part of a birthday ritual, and meets a large Minotaur calling himself the Beast Master. Albert discovers from the friendly Beast Master that he is not from Earth and, with proper training, is capable of transforming his entire body into an animal. He is excited to learn about himself and his abilities, but is very suspicious of his fake Grandparents.

Before he can learn the full details of his discoveries, wolf-like monsters kill Albert's kidnappers. These creatures pursue him across strange and bizarre realms, trying to capture him and return him to his parents. Along the path of escape, he meets a younger brother he didn't know he had, who also was kidnapped, and an older adult friend, Mason.

Mason and his daughter, Lisa, introduce Albert and his brother to a unique way to travel to realms beyond Earth, magically enhanced soda pop cans. He and his brother, Karter, use this method to escape from their Father's men but are eventually captured and returned to their parents.

Both boys experience the evil and meanness of their Father and soon work on a way to escape from their family castle. During their stay, Albert learns the true meaning of his abilities and his destiny as the future ruler of his family's kingdom. The boys plan to escape, but they are caught by their Father and labeled as traitors.

With help from their Mother and friends, Albert and Karter escape to a safe room and are put under the care of Mason as his legal wards. They learn that Lisa is actually their half-sister and that the Mother that they all share is spying on their evil Father to help the Coalition of Good in the other realms.

Albert is overjoyed when he learns that Mason, Lisa, Karter and he are going to be a family, but becomes extremely excited when he also discovers he will be attending the Braunite Beast School. Albert attends his first year at the strange Beast School and uncovers a plot to recycle the children for their youth. They discover that their beloved teacher, Mr. Papaclock, is behind it and develop a plan to rescue the children he has taken, including their friend and housemate, Lisa.

Karter and Albert track the teacher down to his home and after a fierce battle with his large, silver-headed henchmen, are able to free the children and send the evil teacher to the deadly Webnock Realm.

CHAPTER ONE
QUEEN NARA

Queen Nara of the Herionite Realm sat quietly in the large oversized chair near her solid gold bed staring at the artistic designs on the vaulted ceiling of her bedroom. She thought she would be more comfortable on the balcony, but due to her intense fear of heights, she had no desire to look down from the eighth floor of the castle. The height would occupy all of her thoughts, and she wanted to think of nothing but her children.

The gold wrist clock on her left arm seemed to be stuck at five minutes to three in the afternoon for several hours. In reality, she knew that time moving slow was only a perception, but still it seemed to last forever in her mind. Three o'clock meant that she would be able to start her monthly talk with Mason. She could hear about her children and discover what they had been up to since the Beast School broke for summer break.

Knock!
Knock!

A knock at the wooden door of the bedroom broke Queen Nara out of her thought process. Standing up, she stretched and crossed the room.

"Yes," Queen Nara said, swinging the door open softly. "Can I help you?"

"The King has asked that I relay a message to you, Your Highness," a large-eyed soldier said, not looking up at the pale-skinned Queen.

"And what does my husband have to say," the Queen replied, her voice cold and unfeeling.

"King John regrets to report that he has been delayed in the Red Rodent Province, and it will take him another day or two before he will be able to return," the guard responded, nervous with how the Queen might react. He waited for a reply and was quickly relieved when she spoke to him in a soft tone.

"Tell the King to take his time. I have spent this last week alone. What is another day or two?"

"Yes, Your Highness." The guard turned to walk away but stopped when the Queen had not shut the door. He faced her and nervously smiled. "Is there anything else, My Queen?"

"Yes, I think there is," Queen Nara said, curling the corners of her mouth in a subtle smile.

"Tell the King that I was crying hysterically and that I seemed to be very depressed."

"Your Highness?" The guard asked confused. "You want me to lie?"

"Are you questioning me?" The Queen put her hands on her hips. "How do you not know that I wasn't crying mere moments ago?"

"Yes, Your Highness. Sorry, Your Highness. I will tell him."

The guard pivoted on his heel, and then he disappeared down the corridor.

Nara shut the door behind her and looked at

her watch. It was a minute past three. She rushed into the bathroom, locked the door and turned the water on. She let it run in the sink and waited until she was sure it was loud enough to hide her voice. Sitting down in a chair towards the back of the extremely large bathroom, she grabbed a shiny hairbrush off the counter and pulled the pure silver back off of it.

The brush came apart in her hands. She twisted and turned it, revealing a hidden communication device, stored in its handle. After completely disassembling it she touched a small, pin-sized button at the bottom of the brush and a low hum of static erupted. Fiddling with a small dial at the top of the handle, she lowered the sound until she could just barely hear the white noise.

"This is Mole to Shadow. Come in Shadow," the Queen said into her hairbrush. There was no response so she repeated her call. "I say again. This is Mole to Shadow, come in."

"Shadow here," a voice responded. It was distorted by a sound disguiser and reminded the Queen of someone talking under water. But she could still recognize the voice of her ex-husband, Mason. "You're late. Is everything okay with the King gone?"

"My apologies," the Queen replied. "I was interrupted by one of the King's guards. We should be fine to talk freely now."

"Understood," the voice said. "What do you have to report?"

"Nothing since last time we talked. It appears that King John has been having trouble conquering the Red Rodent Province."

"Your information helped us prepare its people

for battle. The Realm Regal has committed two battalions of our troops in disguise. I think your King will return home with a loss."

"Good," Nara said, a smile forming on her face. "Now on to some more important things. How are Lisa, Albert and Karter doing?"

"They are fine. The second year of school was finished with no incidents or attacks. As far as the summer, I was actually surprised, but it seems that Lisa convinced the boys to go to the Dsertian Realm with her. She gave the trip to Albert for his twelfth birthday present."

"Why in the world would they want to go to that dry, dirty place?"

"This last year at school they became very chummy with a child from that Realm, and since the boys were still getting used to all of the different cultures, Lisa thought it would be a good idea to be in the desert - to help broaden their minds."

"Is she still giving you problems?"

"Nothing I can't handle. Lisa is very strong-willed, but I got used to that with you when we were still married. You know, she is very much like you."

"Thank you, I think. I wish we could tell her that I am her Mother, and I wish I could be there for her, but it would ..."

"You can't. We need you to continue to spy for the Coalition and pretend to be with King John for at least another year. But soon, I promise."

"Tell them I miss them," Queen Nara said, tears forming in the corners of her eyes.

"We miss you, too," Mason replied, slightly choked up himself. "Maybe when this is all over, we can reevaluate our feelings."

"I'd like that," Queen Nara replied. "I should go; too much time on the line, and they might be able to trace it back to me."

"Agreed. Take care of yourself, and I will talk to you next month."

"You, too. Bye." The line went dead and the Queen cried. She put her brush back together and wiped the tears from her face.

Queen Nara had just wiped the last trace of water from her cheek when a loud crash in her bedroom startled her. Quickly, she unlocked the door and stepped out of the bathroom. She scanned the room, but could see nothing out of place. Turning her attention towards the balcony, she quietly gasped as the shadows of several men crossed back and forth behind the drape.

"Who is there?" she ordered, ready to defend herself if one of her husband's men heard a portion of the conversation and attempted to arrest her.

The shade to the balcony began to rise as five figures stepped in through the open door. They pushed the curtain to the side and revealed themselves.

The five figures were dressed in similar, ragged, blue uniforms with a red bandanna around the top of their heads and large swords strapped around their waists. They each had long hair, dark-tanned skin, and unkempt beards that grew wildly in all directions. One had an eye patch over his left eye and two others had large scars stretching across their faces.

"What are you doing in the royal palace?" Queen Nara asked, anger and fear in her voice. "You have violated many laws just by being here."

Prince Albert, Book 3: The Realm Pirates

The man with the eye patch stepped forward and smiled, revealing several missing teeth. "I am First Mate Kos of the People's Association of Piracy from the ship, the Dutchman, and you are my prisoner."

"How did you get in here? Guards!" Nara screamed, stepping back.

"Get her!" Kos ordered. "The Captain doesn't want any alarms."

The four men rushed across the room on command while their leader with the eye patch watched. Nara ducked to the side and kicked out with her extended left leg. Her nicely fashioned boot connected with the side of one of the scarred man's head. He flipped over and rolled to the right, holding his head in extreme agony.

During this maneuver, the Queen didn't notice another scarred man coming up from behind her. He reached around her neck and squeezed in an attempt to control her. Nara leaned forward against the man's strong grip and turned her attacker's weight against him. She flipped him forward causing him to collide with another Pirate rushing towards her.

The fourth Pirate had already drawn his sword and stepped in front of the Queen. He thrust his sword towards Nara and motioned for her to stop fighting. She, however, took it as a challenge and rolled towards him. The back of her left foot collided with the surprised Pirate's left hand and sent his long blade spiraling through the air. She completed the roll and found herself face to face with the disarmed man. Not giving him time to react, she lashed out and punched the man in his throat. Gasping for air, the Pirate staggered back and tripped over one of the scarred men.

"You're next," Queen Nara said, turning back towards First Mate Kos.

"I have to admit I am impressed, but I don't think we will be leaving without you. Put your hands in the air," Kos replied, drawing an old-style gun from his belt. The men on the ground began to stand. "Would you fools get up? If the Captain saw you he would be furious. One of you put the shackles on her."

Queen Nara stood helpless as the Pirates circled her. She couldn't move faster than a bullet. They pulled her hands down and clasped them behind her back with large metal rings around her wrists. They tested to make sure she couldn't break free, and when satisfied that she was secure, led her out to the balcony.

All of the questions that Nara had about how the men had entered her room undetected were immediately answered. Floating several feet from the balcony and eight stories in mid-air, a large sailing ship blocked out the view of the sun. It had three tall masts that held sails larger than the Queen had ever seen, with a tattered, black, skull-and-crossbones flag blowing softly from the center mast. The model of a large eagle sat attached to the front part of the ship giving the appearance that the boat was three feet longer than it actually was.

Nara couldn't believe what she was seeing. Not only should the ship not be there, but also the Pirates had placed a wooden plank from the ship to her balcony and had entered her room from across it. She hadn't seen a ship like this since the war with the Realm Pirates twenty years prior. But the Realm

Prince Albert, Book 3: The Realm Pirates

Pirates had supposedly all been killed or captured. What she was seeing was impossible? But there it was in front of her.

"I see our ship is impressive to you," Kos said, pushing Nara out on to the plank.

"You're Realm Pirates," Nara replied, nervously looking down at the ground below her. The shakiness of the board amplified her fear of heights. It wasn't until she had safely made it to the ship before she turned back to Kos and asked, "Are you Realm Pirates?"

Kos smiled, showing the Queen his missing tooth grin. "Yes. We are the Realm Pirates, and we *are* back. This way. The Captain wants to see you."

The large sailing ship floated away from the balcony and into the open blue sky. Its large sails filled with wind and carried Queen Nara away from the safety of her castle.

CHAPTER TWO
THE DSERTIAN REALM

"Tell me again, why are we spending our summer break in the desert?" Albert asked, pulling his tired feet in and out of the deep sand.

"Because it was a birthday present, and you are doing this to help improve your knowledge of other realms," Lisa replied, adjusting the collar of the oversized, hooded robe she wore. The cloak was identical to those worn by the other travelers. It was designed to shield them from the sun and to control the sweat within their body. Becoming dehydrated in the middle of the desert was never a good thing. "And to make sure that you embrace diversity instead of gawking at different people in uneducated amazement."

"I don't gawk."

"You gawk," Lisa replied, picking up the pace and walking faster. "Let's catch up to Karter and Tito. We wouldn't want them to think we weren't enjoying ourselves, would we?"

"Great." Albert started walking quicker, but found it hard to keep up. Eventually he caught up to Lisa, Tito and his brother.

"So, Albert, how are you liking your birthday

present?" Karter asked, smiling. He knew his brother was miserable.

"Oh, it's great," Albert lied, knowing that Tito would be hurt at any other answer."

In two more months, when I turn ten and get my beast face, we will have to come back again. Can you arrange that, Lisa?" Karter shot a grin to the only girl of the group.

"I'm sure I can arrange it." Lisa patted Albert on the shoulder, taking a small pleasure in his having to hide his misery.

Albert nodded and the four continued on, paying careful attention not to open their mouths as a dust cloud blew by. The cloud passed and he yawned stretching the dry corners of his mouth. In complete silence, the four hikers marched to the top of the sandy dune and looked out at the shiny, light-brown sand in front of them. The way it reflected the light from the three suns in the sky gave it a bright glow that seemed nothing short of angelic.

"I never imagined that it could be this beautiful," Karter commented, taking a drink from the large canteen he carried over his shoulder. "Thank you for inviting us to your realm."

"You are my friends. It would be a shame to hide this. I am sorry the walk is so tiring. The Sand Sea is just something that can't be missed. Sorry, about it being so hot," Tito said. The soft-spoken boy had earned the reputation as *Mr. Sorry* because of his continuous need to apologize.

"Please stop apologizing," Lisa said. "I thought we talked about you working on that. You don't want people to call you *Mr. Sorry* forever, do you?"

"Sorry, you're right. I will work on it." Tito smiled, realizing he apologized again. "How about in the future we put a soda can out here? That way we don't have to walk. It would be much easier that way," Albert commented.

"Don't listen to him," Lisa said, taking a drink from her canteen. The water soothing her dry throat was refreshing and filled her with more energy. "The view is worth the walk."

"Besides," Tito added. "If we put a can out here, then people could transport whenever they want to, and the area could get ruined. My people want to preserve the beauty as long as possible. But I am sorry about ..." Tito stopped himself in mid-apology. He really did want to stop saying sorry; he just found it hard not to feel responsible for the things around him.

"I notice a large black dot at the bottom of the other hill," Karter said. "What is that?"

"That's a rock formation. It is gold-diamond rock. Worthless to sell, but very beautiful."

"It can't be more than half a mile or so away. Let's walk down and see it," Lisa said, starting down the hill. As she passed Albert, she flashed him a sarcastic smile.

"Yeah, great," Albert replied, following her down. He could feel the sand in his shoes squish between his toes. His only thought was of how much he hated the dirt. Why couldn't they have come to a water world or something? Why did it have to be the desert? He muttered, "No better sight than a worthless piece of rock named after a couple of priceless ones."

The four children continued their hike down into the valley of the Sand Sea. They had only traveled a quarter of a mile when Karter noticed a small pool of red liquid slowly being absorbed into the sand.

"Tito, what's this?" Karter asked, leaning down to the strange, crimson fluid.

Tito couched next to him and poked his finger into the red liquid. He swirled his finger around and then brought it up to his nose and smelled it. His eyes filled with panic as he quickly turned in a circle scanning the area around him. He was searching for something?

"What is it?" Lisa asked.

"We have to get out of here, quick!" Tito exclaimed, continuing to spin in a circle scanning the sand around them. "Run for the rock formation!"

"Why? What's going on?" Albert asked.

"Sand sharks will be coming soon. They can't get us on the rocks."

"Whoa, whoa. What are sand sharks?" Karter asked, intrigued.

"We can talk about this later," Tito shouted. "Run, before it's too late."

Without further explanation the four children ran for the rock formation. It was still a quarter of a mile away and their pace slowed as they became more and more tired. Along the entire way, Tito continued to demand that his friends keep running swiftly. All of their lives depended on it.

"What's that?" Karter asked, pointing to a silver, triangular shape moving down the hill towards them.

"It's a sand shark!" Tito screamed in terror. "You all are too far away. We aren't going to make it, and I can't protect you."

"Look," Karter said, pointing to the top of the hill. "There are two more of those things coming this way. What do we do?"

Albert stepped forward and put his hand on Tito's shoulder. He made eye contact with his friend and tried to help him focus. "Stay with me Tito. You said that you can't protect us. Can you get away from them? Can you get to safety?"

"Yes. My people have the ability to glide through the sand. But I can't bring anyone with me."

"Go, then. We will meet you at the rocks."

"I won't leave you."

"We will be fine," Albert said, flashing a fake, half-smile. Tito looked toward Karter and Lisa. They nodded in agreement. Tito turned and melted into the sand. His entire body shifted into grains of dirt and merged with the dune. Where their friend once stood, the kids only saw a dark-colored pile of sand and empty clothes. The pile began to shift and merge with the rest of the dune. It disappeared in the mass. Tito had moved on as he was asked. Karter leaned down and picked up the pile of empty clothes for his friend.

"Lisa, take Karter," Albert ordered.

Without hesitation, Lisa began the transformation of her upper body. The features of a bird morphed into her face, and two large wings jutted out of her back and through her cloak, forming a beautiful spread of feathers. Within seconds, a beautiful half-bird, half-human, stood majestically on the sand. She grasped Karter tightly in her arms and leapt high into the air.

"Wait just a minute!" Karter exclaimed as he was carried away. "We can't leave Albert behind."

"He will be fine," Lisa responded through her now beaked mouth.

Prince Albert, Book 3: The Realm Pirates

Albert turned back towards the oncoming sharks. He made sure that Lisa and Karter were out of the rushing attacker's way before he continued his sprint towards the rocks. Continually looking over his shoulder, he watched to see if the sharks were getting any closer. He could tell very quickly that, as a boy, he would not be able to avoid them. He was going to have to transform. Without having a change of clothes with him, he wished there was another option, but the intense situation left him no other choices.

Albert mentally signaled the change in his body. He had never done it on the run before. His skin started to bubble and stretch in various directions as it grew and reshaped itself. The clothes on his back ripped and fell to the side as his growing body could no longer be contained within them. The paws of a lion were noticeable first on the bubbling body. He dropped to the ground on all fours. At first it was difficult to run, but as his arms stretched to match his back legs, the strides became easier and the pace quickened. Albert's head enlarged next and grew the golden hair of a lion's mane. The whole frame of his body took on a new structure. The remaining pieces of his clothes fell to the dirt, and yellowish-brown hair spread wildly across his new torso. Where once Albert had been, now stood a lion four times the size of the young boy.

Off in the distance, Albert, the Lion, could see Lisa land on the rock formation with his brother. He looked behind him and stopped when he could no longer see the fins of the three sharks. Had they gone away? Had Tito worried for nothing?

"Don't stop," Tito yelled as his body reformed from the grains of dirt on the rock formation. Lisa and

Karter were startled by the sudden reappearance of their friend. "They are still there. Run!"

"Didn't you hear him? Run!" Karter echoed, handing Tito the clothes he had picked up.

Albert wasn't sure how Tito knew, but he trusted him. He leapt from his spot on the sand just as the large, open mouth of a sand shark burst from the ground beneath him. It had barely missed him, but gave the lion a full view of what was chasing them.

The sand shark was forty feet in length. It was gray with a large mouth full of four rows of teeth. Like the water sharks from the Earth Realm, it had large gill-type ridges down both of its sides, probably for breathing under sand. Its large, oversized eyes followed Albert through the air and to a patch of sand several yards away.

Albert realized that there were two more sand sharks out there, just like this one. That hard fact flooded adrenalin through the lion and caused him to increase his speed once he landed. Several more feet passed beneath him before he fell, grumbling in the sand. An instinct inside of him said to leap into the air. So leap he did and thanked that voice as a second sand shark burst from the dirt, its mouth clamping open and closed. From high above, he looked into the mouth of the sand shark and shuddered at the terrifying jaws full of sharp teeth, chomping for his bones.

As Albert descended towards the ground, he found the third shark waiting for him. Its mouth was wide open and patiently waited for him to land. Flipping in mid air, Albert positioned his body to land on the back of the third sand shark. He released his claws and angled his paws down.

Landing on top of the sand shark, Albert, the Lion, dug his claws deep into the back of the carnivorous beast. It screamed in agony and wiggled away from the lion. The shark disappeared in the sand and left Albert alone. Not taking any additional chances, Albert bolted for the rock formation.

"That was close," Albert, the Lion, responded through clenched teeth, as he climbed onto the solid ground with his brother and friends. "I thought for sure that last one would have gotten me."

"Why didn't you warn us about those?" Lisa asked, mentally signaling the retraction of her beast face. The bird facial features and wings disappeared, and the young girl remained. Unlike Albert, her clothes were undamaged except on two spots where the wings had sprouted from her back.

"I am so sorry," Tito said, truly meaning to apologize. Sand sharks don't attack people. It wasn't something I thought would be a danger."

"Well, those three attacked," Albert, the Lion, said, between heavy breaths.

"That was a different circumstance," Tito explained." Someone must have specifically drawn those sand sharks to us."

"What do you mean, drew them to us?" Lisa asked. "I don't understand."

"That liquid. It was blood. Freshly poured from the look of it. The fluid hadn't been completely absorbed, so it couldn't have been there longer than an hour. The sand sharks can smell blood ten miles away. It sent them into a frenzy and drew them to us."

"But who would do that?" Karter asked.

"Someone who knew what blood would do to the sand sharks," King John Herionite said, stepping into view on a rock several feet above the children.

"You," Albert the Lion, roared.

"Easy, Son," the King cautioned. "I had to make sure that you hadn't gone weak on me. By the way, happy twelfth birthday and a happy almost tenth to you, Karter. Soon you will get that beast face. I can't wait to see what it is you become."

"Stop trying to pretend you care," Albert, the Lion, roared. "What is the meaning of this? Why did you try to kill us?"

"Kill *you*?" the King was shocked. "I didn't really care about the others, but I knew you would survive my little test."

"Test!" Karter exclaimed. "We could have all been killed."

"I was confident that Albert would survive. I have need of his help."

"You have a funny way of asking for it," Albert, the Lion, said. "Even before this stunt, what makes you think I would help do anything for you?"

"Because it isn't for me. It's for your Mother. She needs your help."

"With what?"

"She has been kidnapped, and the ransom note says that, if I try to rescue her, they will kill her. So that leaves you as her only hope."

CHAPTER THREE
THE PIRATES' LIFE

The Pirates worked feverishly across the deck of their ship, the Dutchman. They prepared the wooden vessel as it slowly lowered its massive bulk into the crystal blue waters of the great ocean of the Amphibia Realm. Upon seeing the large, Brigantine type ship flying through the air, most people assumed it wasn't seaworthy - but not the Dutchman. She handled equally well in the air or in the water.

"All stop," yelled the ambitious First Mate, Kos. He walked proudly across the main deck of the ship, smiling at the smooth-running vessel. He did so love to see a well-trained crew. "Secure all moorings and prepare for smooth ocean sailing. Upon splash down, I want forward movement as quick as possible." The orders flew instinctively from the lips of Kos. He had been doing his job for many years and hoped some day it would earn him command of his own ship.

"Aye, Aye," the Pirate crew responded in unison.

"I want a man in the crow's nest at all times to keep watch for approaching ships. Our precious cargo will bring a multitude of buyers our way; we wouldn't want them sneaking up on us. The Captain and I will be in the hold with our lovely prisoner."

The Pirates grunted in sadistic pleasure and followed the First Mate's orders to the letter. As ropes were tied and sails unfurled, a tall, bone-skinny man with large eyes grabbed hold of the rope ladder connected to the center mast and began to climb to the lookout point, high in the air. The wind blew his body from side to side, but the dedicated Pirate continued his ascent. Within a few minutes, he settled into the round, tight-fitting crow's nest and watched the water around him. He was ready for whatever might come.

Queen Nara sat quietly in the hold of the ship just below the main deck. The barred room served as the ship's brig and, as such, was very cramped and dirty. The Queen had to fight down the bile in the back of her throat as the smell of mold and decaying food filled her nostrils. If later asked, she would claim the smell was the worst part of her abduction.

The darkness of the below-ship area kept her from determining a way to escape. Eventually, they would come see her, and when they did, she was confident they would have some kind of light, and she would spy a way out. She would *not* be used as a hostage. She had a mission to fulfill for the Coalition, and she wanted to complete it and get home to her children and her first love, Mason.

As the ship sat down in the water, another inconvenience presented itself to Nara's situation. Two small leaks had formed between three wood flats in the bottom corner of her cell causing the dirt and grime to be mixed with a few inches of sea water.

Prince Albert, Book 3: The Realm Pirates

Small beams of light shone through the holes giving her enough sight to see the resulting mud and greenish colored liquid.   Nara climbed on her bunk and sat perched with her legs curled up to her chest.

The hatch above the dingy hold opened up, flooding the room with the bright rays of the sun. Nara was instantly blinded. A few moments passed. Her eyes adjusted, and for the first time in the several hours since her capture, she could see around the room that was her cage. Across the way from her cell, she noticed an identical barred room. Laid out across the bed was a thick, white-haired man with ragged clothes and chains around his wrists and ankles. She hadn't heard him move in the darkness and wondered if he was dead or alive. Perhaps he was the smell that was so offending.

"Hello there," Queen Nara called out. "Are you alive?"

The white-haired man didn't respond.

"Don't bother," Kos said, climbing down the stairs of the open hatch.   "The Captain's Father stopped talking years ago. But you can trust me when I tell you, that old coot is still alive and with us." He rubbed the patch across his eye indicating the old man as the reason it was gone.

"The Captain's Father?" Queen Nara responded in shock. "He keeps his Father caged?"

"He's not a good man," A voice replied from behind Kos. Stepping into the hatch's open light, the figure became instantly recognized by Nara. The large, burly man with curly, red hair and a bright-red beard, removed his Captain's hat and ducked into the hold. On the left shoulder of his perfectly-shaped, black jacket sat a blue, two-headed parrot.

"So, you are the Captain?" Nara stated, disgust and anger in her voice.

"I am," replied the broad-shouldered man, adjusting the perfect fitting, black pants. "Captain Van Decken at your service." The Captain bowed, almost causing the quiet parrot to fall from his shoulder.

Nara stared at the sharply-dressed man and marveled at how clean his white, sparkling shirt and pressed uniform were. Compared to the dirty, faded clothes of his First Mate, the Captain looked like a king. *But he wasn't,* Nara told herself. He was a terrorist that could fake being polite, but in the end he would gladly trade her life for a few dollars.

"If you should need anything to make your stay with us more comfortable, please do not hesitate to ask one of our maids or friendly service men." The Captain smirked at his own joke.

"You think you're funny?" Queen Nara asked, rolling her eyes.

"I do find myself quite humorous at times," Captain Van Decken replied.

"I don't think you understand the situation you are in. Kidnapping is an offense punishable by death in the Herionite realm. And if my husband gets hold of you first, you can add torture and misery to that punishment." Queen Nara stopped talking as she watched the two-headed parrot change from blue to purple. The unusual bird watched her with both sets of its eyes.

"Oh, I understand the situation quite clearly. You are my prisoner and quite frankly, you are worth quite a bit of money. And yes, my men and I realize that death is a possibility, but very unlikely. I have it on good authority that, even as we speak, your precious husband is gathering the money I asked for and will soon make a delivery."

"You couldn't be more wrong," Nara snapped. "He is figuring out how to kill you. And I can't wait until you two meet."

The parrot changed from purple to red. At first it was a light-red, but gradually got darker as each second passed. Nara had never seen such an unusual bird and wondered where he came from.

"You listen to me!" the Captain yelled. "I am not about to let some pampered royalty do anything to me or my ship. I had thought about turning you over unharmed when we got our money, but now I think you may need to come to some harm before that."

"It appears that I have offended you," Nara responded, her voice soft and cordial. She wanted to keep her captor emotionally upset and, somewhere deep inside, was enjoying this little game. "I apologize, Captain Van Decken. I merely stated the facts."

"The Captain is a smart man. He will not fall for your fake apologies," Kos said, looking to his Captain for confirmation.

"Yes," the Captain replied, his breathing slowing. "I do not trust you, my dear. Your apology is accepted, but you need to watch your tongue. I will think about our little conversation, and perhaps I will change my mind and not harm you. We shall see."

Queen Nara watched the bird slowly return to a blue tint. She watched to see if it would change again, but it maintained its blue hue. The Captain stared at her, not saying a word. He followed her gaze to the two-headed parrot and smiled.

"I see you like me parrot," Captain Van Decken said, as his voice returned to his calm and even tone. "His name is Bip."

"Why does it keep changing colors?"

"This is a very special bird, and smart as well. It is a mood parrot. While he is on my shoulder, the color of his feathers matches my emotion. If I was very angry, it would be red, blue if I was calm, green for envy, and so on."

"It's amazing."

"I would agree. The bird is quite unique."

"No, not the bird," Queen Nara said, a smile forming on her lips. "You."

The Captain looked confused. He turned to Kos, and his First Mate shrugged his shoulders in confusion as well. He turned back to Nara. "I don't understand what do you mean, *me*."

"Here you are a Captain of your own ship, and not only do you keep your old Father locked up below, but you play with birds. What's next, dressing up and playing with dolls? Perhaps if you like, we can go back to my castle and get some make-up."

The parrot became instantly red. It looked like it was on fire. Nara made no attempt to hide her pleasure, as a large smile spread across her face. She now knew how to push his buttons. It was easy to see the things that would anger Captain Van Decken and the way to calm him down. She would patiently wait and see how she could use that information. Some of the control had shifted back to her; the Captain just didn't know it.

Without saying a word, Captain Van Decken

spun on the heels of his shiny boots and climbed up the steps to the main deck.

"You have just made a big mistake," Kos said, staring at the Queen in utter contempt. "This could have gone easy on you. But your mouth will make sure you aren't treated right."

"I'm sorry," Queen Nara replied. "I hadn't realized that my cell was the top accommodation around here. What do you sleep in, a puddle?"

"Keep talking. You run your mouth much more, and you can guarantee yourself death."

Kos climbed the steps of the hold and slammed the hatch down behind him. The room once again filled with darkness.

CHAPTER FOUR
REVELATIONS

"He did what? Mason exclaimed, sweat forming on his bald, blue head. His massive shoulders tensed with stress and anger. He couldn't believe what he was hearing.

"He asked for our help with the Realm Pirates," Albert responded.

"No, no. Not that. He sent three sand sharks after you?"

"Not exactly," Karter added. "He just poured the blood in the sand. The sharks came on their own after that."

Mason looked at Karter. His eyes said what his mouth did not. He didn't want any interference from the boy. Turning back to Albert, he said, "I just can't believe he would do that. He put you all in danger. Don't take this the wrong way, but your Father is a madman. Do you know that?"

"Kind of got a clue with the whole *trying to execute me thing* a while back."

"Okay, good point. It's shocking, but I will put that aside for now. You said he asked you to help with the Realm Pirates?"

"Yes."

"What kind of help? I didn't think they existed anymore. The Realm Pirates haven't shown their faces since the Three Year War. When they were defeated, they blended back into society and their organization all but disappeared."

"Well, they're back, I guess, and he wants me to help him get back what they took."

"Why are you being so vague about this, Albert? You are normally more open. So out with it, what did they take from your Father?"

"Are you sure you want to know?"

"Albert?" Mason crossed his arms and leaned toward the small boy.

"Maybe you should sit down."

"Out with it!" Mason screamed.

"My Mother."

"Okay, what did they take from your Mother?"

"No, Mason, you don't understand." Albert's eyes met Mason's. "That's what they took from him, my Mother. Queen Nara has been kidnapped from the castle, and they want a ransom for her."

Mason dropped down into a chair. He lowered his head between his legs and took in deep breaths. He had talked with her the previous day. They had become much closer than they had been when they were married. They had high hopes of being together again. How could it all be threatened so easily?

"Told you to sit down," Albert said, squinting his eyes.

Albert and Karter stared at him, not sure what to do. They tried to look below his crouched-over body, but his face was hidden from view. Was he crying? They couldn't tell.

Lisa walked down the stairs and stepped into the living room. She immediately could feel that something was wrong. After seeing her Dad bent over, she immediately rushed to his side.

"What is it?" Lisa asked.

"Nothing, Honey," Mason replied, wiping his strong hands against his cheeks and eyes. He took a deep breath and stood up. "I have to go out for a little bit, but I will be back soon."

"Where are you going?" Albert asked, concerned for their mentor and legal guardian. "I am going to go the Realm Regal and see about getting back Queen Nara."

"King John said that he didn't send his ships after them, because he was afraid they might kill her. If you tell the Realm Regal, they might do the same thing. And then ..."

"Albert, you know that I don't want any harm to come to Nara. I will do everything I can to make sure she is rescued safely. But if your Father was right and the Realm Pirates have your Mom, she is in danger every second I delay."

Mason grabbed his coat off the back of the couch and started for the front door. "Did he have any idea where they were, when he last checked?"

"He said somewhere in the Amphibia Realm, but with them moving so quickly, he wasn't sure how long they would be there."

Mason opened the front door, then stopped and faced the children. "I don't want you three doing anything stupid. The Realm Pirates are not to be messed with. They are nasty cutthroats. I want you to promise me you will not go anywhere near them."

"We promise," Lisa said. "Are you sure you don't want me to go with you?"

"I'll be back soon." Mason left and shut the door behind him.

"We told him about the Realm Pirates taking our Mom," Karter commented after seeing the concern and confusion on Lisa's face.

"I have never seen my Dad that upset before. I know that Nara is your Mom and a loyal member of the Coalition, but I don't understand my Dad's strong emotion." Lisa said, plopping down on the lime- green couch. "He was actually crying."

"You'd think he was in love with her or something," Karter remarked. He realized what he had said a second too late and clasped his hand over his mouth.

"Karter!" Albert said, angry.

"What do you two know?" Lisa asked, her eyes darting between the two boys.

"Nothing," Karter responded. "I don't know what you're talking about."

"I can tell you two are hiding something. You were never good liars."

"I am too," Karter exclaimed, realizing the nature of his statement a second too late. "Well, you know what I mean."

"Out with it?"

Karter looked nervously at Albert and back to Lisa. "We can't."

"You can and you will," Lisa demanded, placing her hands on her hips. "Otherwise, life will get very difficult around here."

"Good job, Karter," Albert said, motioning for Lisa to sit down. "Sit down with me, and I will explain. But you have to promise me you won't tell anyone that you know about it."

"About what?" Lisa asked, sitting down next to Albert. "Tell me."

"The truth is," Albert began. "You and Karter and I are more than just house mates."

"Yeah, we are good friends," Lisa commented. "But that's not what you mean, is it?"

"We are related," Albert blurted out. "You are our sister."

Lisa's eyes darted back and forth trying to absorb the knowledge. She smiled. "Come on! Really?"

"Really." Albert's face was stone cold and all serious.

"If we are brother and sister, then that means that Queen Nara is my ... Mother."

"Bingo," Karter said, sitting on the arm rest of the couch.

"Then my Dad was with ..."

"Mason and our Mother were married for several years. They had a rough time and split up. Shortly after that, she met and married our Father. When she saw the level of his evil, she became an agent for the Coalition and she has been working for our side ever since."

"But why would my Father keep this from me? Why would he lie to me?"

"It's complicated. I am not sure how it all works, but if our Father knew you existed, he would try to get you as well. As the female heir, you would be more valuable than us. I guess the women inherit all the money and stuff, not the men."

"This is too much to take in," Lisa commented,

leaning back on the couch. "How could this be kept from me all of these years?"

"It was for your protection," Albert interjected. "They both love you very much, and I think they love each other, from everything we've seen."

"He's right," Karter added. "And the only reason we know is we found out their secret when we were prisoners in Dad's castle. Otherwise they wouldn't have told us, either."

"My Mother is alive," Lisa mumbled, a smile forming on her face. "I can't wait to talk to her. It will be so cool to ..."

"Whoa," Albert said, raising his hand up. "You can't tell anyone."

"But ..."

"You promised. If anyone found out, you would be in incredible danger."

"But ..."

"No one," Karter added.

"Alright, but it just doesn't seem fair. My Mom is alive, and I can't tell her I know."

"Someday you will, just not today," Albert replied. "So we need to figure out how we are going to get our Mom back."

"I am sure the Realm Regal will help."

"Me too, but something inside tells me they will send everything they have after them. My Father is many things, but stupid isn't one of them. He would have sent all of his ships if he thought it would have worked. I think we all know that if we want to get her back safely, it has to be the three of us to do it."

"I promised my Dad that we would not go near the Pirates."

"*You* promised," Karter added, offering a sly smirk. "Not *us.*"

"Just like I keep my promise to you, I want to keep it to him. After that incident with Mr. Papaclock, he hasn't fully trusted any of us. He used to trust me with everything. I want to get some of that back. And lying to him isn't the way."

Lisa jumped off the couch and headed back up the stairs.

"Where are you going?" Karter asked.

"I'm going to go look through some of the old photo boxes in the attic and see if they have any with my Mom and Dad." Lisa disappeared at the top of the stairs a moment later.

"She's going to be a problem," Karter said, sure that Lisa was out of listening range. "What are we going to do?"

"Well, you were the one who let it slip."

"What were we supposed to do? You know as well as I do that she would have hounded us until we told her. But what are we going to do about Mom? I think you were right; we have to do something."

"I have an idea," Albert said, a frown on his face. "But it could be very dangerous for you. I would do it myself, but I have become too well known."

"Dangerous, hmmm. That sounds great," Karter replied, excited. "So, big brother, what is it you would like me to do?"

CHAPTER FIVE
THE REALM REGAL

After enduring almost an hour of security checks and questions from guards posted at every door and gate, Mason finally made it to the Realm Regal's building. He was aware for the need to protect the leader of all realms, but on a day he was in a hurry, it was an inconvenience that was just barely tolerable.

Climbing the huge marble steps, two at a time, Mason made his way through the pure-white pillars and to the entrance of the majestic, three-story building. Standing in front of the main double doors was another Regal guard. His blue, flowing robe and tall, black hat waggled as the sentry snapped to attention and raised his sword towards Mason.

"I'm here to see the Realm Regal," Mason said, his voice slightly elevated.

"Do you have an appointment?" the guard asked, making eye contact with Mason.

"I will tell you what I told the other ten guards that have asked me the same question. I do not have an appointment. This is an emergency, and I need to speak to her about one of our undercover operatives. My security access code is YTR419."

The guard scanned a small computer pad in his right hand. He found the code and compared the picture to the blue-skinned man in front of him. Satisfied it was a match, the guard stepped to the side and said, "It checks out. You may enter. Have a nice day and pleasant visit, Agent Mason."

"Blow it out your ear, you polter." Mason stormed past the man.

"How rude," the guard replied, shocked by the hostile comment.

Mason closed the red doors behind him and crossed the large lobby. Several diplomats and dignitaries were talking in various small gatherings of chairs and little tables. They paid no attention to him as he made his way to the stairs and climbed them rapidly to the next floor. He entered the second floor landing and jogged down the hallway to the last office on the left.

"May I help you?" a yellow-tinted man asked, seeing Mason enter the room.

"I am here to see the Realm Regal!" Mason shouted, leaning in closer to the green-suited assistant. "Tell her Mason is here."

"Do you have an appointment?" the assistant replied, straightening the green, polka dot tie that was one shade lighter than his suit.

"No, I do not have an appointment!" Mason yelled, a red tint glowing on his dark blue skin. "Why does everyone keep asking me that?"

"Without an appointment, no one sees ..."

"I need to see her now."

"I'm sorry, but ..."

"It's okay, Deg," a soft voice said from behind.

Both men looked up and smiled at the magnificent form of the Realm Regal. They stared at her beautiful facial features and her remarkable clothing. The Realm Regal was wearing a dark-red, sparkling dress that fluffed out with a glow at the shoulders and at the waist. It hung low on her neck and flowed from top of her shoulders all the way to the floor. She had long, flowing, light-red hair that curled around her pale-colored body twice and accented the dress color perfectly.

"Are you sure?" the assistant asked. "I could call a guard, and we could have him removed."

Mason moved towards Deg. He was in no mood to be insulted. But he stopped himself before acting. There were more important things to do than worry about his pride.

"We have nothing to fear from one of our top operatives," the Realm Regal said, smiling to reveal strong, white teeth between her ruby-red lips. "Please hold all of my calls."

"Thank you," Mason replied, heading towards her office. "And I am sorry I yelled at Deg. This is a matter of life and death."

Deg didn't respond. He watched Mason follow the Realm Regal into her office and close the door behind them. Turning back to his work, the yellow assistant began typing on his computer and cursing Mason beneath his breath.

"So, Mason, what is the emergency?" the Realm Regal asked, settling in the large, wood chair behind her shiny, black desk.

"It's Nara. The Realm Pirates have her," Mason replied, trying to calm himself.

"The Realm Pirates? I thought they were all but extinct. We haven't heard from them in over twenty years. Are you sure?"

"As sure as we can be. King John, himself, surprised Albert in the Dsertian Realm and gave him the information."

"King John? As in King John, the Dark Red, of the Herionite Realm - the sworn enemy to the Coalition and the murderer of thousands."

"I know how this sounds," Mason replied, motioning for the Regal to listen. "But please, you have to listen. The threat is real."

"I think it's *you* who needs to do the listening," the Regal said, her voice becoming cold and stern. "This man is one of the most untrustworthy in all of the realms. This is probably some elaborate plan for him to get the boys back."

"I thought about that. But he had the chance to get the boys in the Dsertian Realm and he didn't. Also, on the way over here, I confirmed with one of our other agents that indeed the Queen is not in the palace and that King John is in the process of gathering a large sum of money to pay the ransom."

"Let's just say you are right, and I am not saying you are, but let's just pretend. If you are right and John is paying the ransom, then why not wait and she will be returned safely."

"With all due respect," Mason bellowed, trying to control his anger. "The Realm Pirates have never done anything by the book. They are notorious for double-crossing people. Not to mention how much King

John loves his money. I am just afraid that they will double-cross each other and Nara will be caught in the middle."

"I understand your concern. But without more information, I am not sure what we can do." The Realm Regal stood and walked to the large, oval widow overlooking the river flowing by her building. She stared solemnly at the rushing water and turned back to Mason. "How about if I launch our own investigation? Once I can confirm this, I will commit our whole fleet to her rescue."

"That is just not good enough. My wife is in danger, and it shocks me that an evil madman like King John seems to care more than you."

"You listen to me," the Realm Regal replied, anger in her voice. "Nara is a loyal agent, and I would protect her to the end of days. But King John can't be trusted. So there will be no help until I know for sure."

"Great!" Mason yelled, standing up and walking towards the door.

"I didn't excuse you."

Mason stopped and faced the Regal. The expression on his face was one of frustration and anger. He wanted to lash out and scream at the world, but deep inside he knew the Regal was right. She couldn't be expected to drop everything for a piece of information from an unreliable source.

"Now, as I was saying," the Realm Regal continued. "I will investigate and let you know what happens. But until then, I do not want you running all over Amphibia trying to find Nara. If she is indeed a prisoner of the Realm Pirates, you may tip them off and cause her to be hurt or worse. I would like you to promise me you will abide by my decision."

Mason didn't answer at first. His thoughts drifted back to the times he had told Lisa, Albert and Karter the same thing. It had to have been just as difficult for them to look him in the eye and lie. "I promise not to go looking for Nara," Mason lied.

"Good. Thank you for bringing this to my attention. You are dismissed."

Mason bowed and headed towards the door.

"And Mason," the Regal called out. "You called Nara *your wife*. Please try to remember that Nara is no longer your wife. And claiming that could put her in more danger with King John. So, I would be careful of what I say if I were you."

Mason grunted in agreement and left the office. The Realm Regal waited until she heard the outer office door shut before pushing the intercom button on her desk. "Deg, come in here, please."

Seconds later, the door to her office opened and her yellow-skinned, green-suited assistant marched in. "Yes, Ma'am."

"I want you to get Captain Antilles on vid-phone for me as soon as possible and set up a face to face meeting with Admiral Nakita."

"Captain Antilles is on drills in the Amphibia Realm, and Admiral Nakita is vacationing in the Fradth Realm. It may take some time."

"I am well aware of their locations," the Realm Regal snapped. "But nevertheless it is important that I talk to them as soon as possible."

"May I at least tell them the subject?"

"Tell them that the Realm Pirates have returned, and they have taken their first victim."

CHAPTER SIX
MASON'S DEPARTURE

Mason threw open the front door of the house scattering the papers Albert and Karter were writing on. Quickly, they hurried to gather the plans they were drawing up and hide them from Mason at the same time.

"It doesn't matter," Mason said, passing through the living room. "I don't have time to see what you are up to anyway. I have to pack."

"Where are you going?" Lisa asked, trotting down the stairs.

"I can't tell you that, Honey," Mason replied, entering his bedroom.

The three children followed him into his downstairs bedroom and watched as he tossed a duffel bag on his unmade bed and began randomly stuffing clothes from his drawers into it.

"Can't we talk about this?" Albert asked, concerned by the frantic behavior of their guardian. "You aren't acting rational."

"Albert, I need you to stay out of this." Mason paused to stare sternly at the young boy, then turned back to his packing.

"At least tell us what the Realm Regal said,"

Karter asked.

"What she said was, *no*," Mason blurted out. He paused, caught his breath and began to pack again. "She said that there was not enough information and that it was probably a trick from your Father. Once again, King John is going to hurt me."

"That's not fair. She has to do more than that," Lisa exclaimed. She wanted to tell Mason that she knew the Queen was her Mother, but her promise to the boys came floating back up to the top of her thoughts.

"They say that they are going to investigate," Mason continued, rushing over to a bare wall opposite his bed. He pushed a hidden button, and the wall slid open revealing weapons and tools of all shapes and sizes. "If they find confirmation, then they will help, but not until then. I have been ordered not to interfere with them."

"So then, why are you packing, Dad?"

"Because I plan on breaking that order. The Regal will no doubt believe that I will not listen to her, and soon I will have someone following me. I have to get going before they can put that person on me."

"Wait a minute," Albert interjected. "When we went against what you said, you got mad at us. How does this make it any different?"

"It doesn't, except that I am the adult and you are to do as I say, not as I do." Mason grabbed a compact bow and arrows, several ropes and metal boxes. He stuffed them into the bag and went back to the hidden wall for more. After a minute, he had the duffel bag packed full and began to zip it up.

"You can't go," Lisa pleaded. "If the Realm Regal

finds you disobeyed her, it will make you a criminal. You will be on the run."

"I have to do this." Mason kissed Lisa on the forehead. "I wish I could tell you something to help you understand, but I can't. This is just something I have to do. I'm sorry, but I have to go." Mason hugged the boys and dragged his bag into the living room.

"How come parents never listen to the kids?" Karter asked.

Mason stopped half way to the door and looked back. "I am truly sorry kids, but I have to go. I will be back soon. In the meantime, I have asked my sister to stop and check on you. I trust you all. Please don't let me down. And if something does happen to me, she will know what to do."

Mason exited the house and was gone. Albert, Karter and Lisa stared at each other in silence. Without a word, Lisa climbed the stairs, entered her room and slammed the door behind her.

"So what do we do now?" Karter asked, throwing his hands in the air.

"Nothing's changed. We follow the plan. With him gone, it might actually be easier. Are you still okay with this?"

"Heck, yeah. I think this idea of yours could really work."

"Good. But before we start this, let's go to my room and use the Remembrance Book."

"That thing your fake Grandparents left you?" Karter asked. "Why?"

"To learn more about the Realm Pirates."

CHAPTER SEVEN
THE REMEMBRANCE BOOK

Albert sat down on the bed with the Remembrance Book on his lap. His mind drifted back to the morning that his Grandparents gave him the book and his life turned upside down.

"So how does this work?" Karter asked, breaking Albert from his trance.

Albert cleared his thoughts and rubbed his hand across the cover remembering that he never did find out what it was made out of. It felt like animal hide, but after all his travels, it was probably an animal he had never seen or heard of. His eyes darted to a large, blue jewel embedded in its center. The jewel was oval shaped and sparkled when the book was held at an angle.

Albert wondered why he hadn't used it since he escaped from the Herionite Realm and his Father. He had put it on the bookshelf shortly after Mason had invited them to stay and never looked at it again. With all of the new experiences rushing his way, it had been easy to forget. After this whole mess was over, he was going to change that. He missed his Grandparents, and with the book, he could at least see his Grandpa anytime he wanted.

Prince Albert, Book 3: The Realm Pirates

"I'm not sure if you will be able to see this or not. How this works is: I rub my finger across the jewel in the center, and visions and memories come back to me."

"Your memories?"

"No, memories left by my Grandfather, verbal messages. I can ask any question, and if he thought to record it, he will answer me."

"Cool," Karter replied, smiling. "Go ahead; let's try it."

Albert cleared his thoughts. Taking a deep breath, he laid the book flat on his lap, focused his mind the best he could and touched the blue stone with his right index finger. He grabbed Karter's hand and placed it on top of his.

"Page one, page one, page one," Albert mumbled as he closed his eyes and concentrated. Images entered Albert's mind. He could see details of things around him and the images made sense. He could see men and women of all shapes, colors and sizes living in realms of all different types. His mind opened up to the diversity that was existence. He saw a realm of water-dwelling creatures. He guessed it was Amphibia, a realm of flying creatures, and he could see a realm of castles and dragons.

"I don't see anything," Karter said, pulling on Albert's arms.

Albert lost concentration and the images faded. "Why did you do that?" Albert yelled, throwing Karter's hand back on his lap.

"I couldn't see anything," Karter replied, confused by his brother's anger.

"I told you that I need to concentrate to make this happen. I will ask the questions and tell you what the answers are when I am done."

"But what I am supposed to do?"

"Go get something to eat, read a book, just don't bother me."

"Fine, I will just lie here." Karter fell back on the bed and stared at the ceiling. He crossed his arms and pouted.

"Fine," Albert replied, focusing back on the book.

"Grandpa, Grandpa, Grandpa."

Albert's Grandfather stepped into view of his mind's eye. Instinctively, he wanted to reach out and grab him, but Albert realized it was all in his head, and it wouldn't do any good. The image of his Grandfather made Albert wish he were real and near enough to hold him. He hadn't realized how much he missed the old man.

The Grandfather image wore a T-shirt, overalls and had a scruffy look about him that made Albert suppose he had just been working in the garden. His Grandfather's image must have been aware of its appearance, because he wet his hand and slicked back his hair. Albert had forgotten what the book had felt like. It was warm and wonderful.

Straightening his clothes, Albert's Grandfather smiled and said," Hello, Albert. How are you?"

"I'm fine," Albert replied. "How are you?"

The image didn't reply. After all, it was only an auto-response to questions, and how would he expect a book to feel?

"I'm sorry," Albert added, realizing his mistake." Please show me everything about the Realm Pirates and what they are."

The image of his Grandfather faded, and his mind

was filled with a soft ocean breeze and ships sailing on the ocean. The Grandfather appeared on one of the ships and smiled. "This is where it all began."

"The pictures are wonderful," Albert replied, trying to be polite to the image. He knew it was not his real Grandpa, but the image just instilled a type of respect for the man. "But I don't need all the details; please, just give me the highlights."

"The Realm Pirates are patterned after the Pirates of Old from the Earth Realm. And as with those original Pirates, the Realm Pirates have similar humble beginnings." His Grandfather paced across the deck of the ship. "Some of the men were deserters from the Realm Navy or ex-military men looking for employment. Many Pirates and Pirate ships came into existence through mutiny. Either way, after the creation of about ten ships, they began to organize. They formed PAP, the Peoples Association of Piracy. Their main purpose was to steal and cause chaos. They began to enlist murderers, career criminals and the worst society had to offer."

"Tell me about the war," Albert asked.

The image shifted to that of ships, sailing across the sea, shooting at each other with large cannons. It reminded Albert of a Pirate movie he had seen a few months before being sucked into the Realms.

"The war began and ended in three years. Based on the internal clock of the Remembrance Book, it appears that the end was about twenty years ago. The war started after a Pirate Captain captured the Realm Regal. He attempted to hold her for ransom, but in the course of her rescue, she was killed."

"But I talked to the Realm Regal?"

"She was succeeded by her daughter, one year later," the image answered.

"Tell me more about the war."

"The death of the Realm Regal caused the war to escalate. It raged on for three bloody years. Both sides took many casualties, but in the end, it was the Realm Pirates who suffered. At the time of their defeat, it was estimated that they had all 340 of their ships and their crews destroyed."

"Well, that is wrong, I happen to know of at least one around," commented Albert.

"Please repeat the question."

"Never mind. What are their ships like?"

"Their ships are made out of wood. The Coalition used steel. The wooden ships are damp, dark and cheerless places. They reek with the stench of bilge water. They always leak and are very difficult to keep dry. It was said that you could not find one ship in which there was a Pirate without a cold or the flu. Below decks, the Pirates would try to fumigate by lighting small fires, but there was too much filth, and rodents would breed there. It was very nasty."

Albert cringed, thinking of his Mother on one of these ships. "What about flight? How do they fly?"

"I have no record of flying ships," the image responded.

"Search for flying ships of any kind."

All was silent for a moment and then the Grandfather image spoke. "There is no reference to any flying sailing ships, Pirate or non-Pirate. There is a rumor and legend of a ghost ship, but it doesn't match the parameters of the search."

"Thank you." Albert removed his finger from the

stone and looked down at his brother, Karter, who was staring at the ceiling. "I have what we need."

Lisa was lying on her bed, almost asleep, when she heard a sudden burst of shouting coming from the hallway outside of her room. She hopped from her bed and stepped into the hall.

"You really can be dumb," Albert yelled, pointing at Karter.

"Well at least I don't rub my hand on a book and make up a bunch of stuff."

"It was real, I told you."

"Stop lying," Karter yelled. "Why can't you just admit you were wrong?"

"I would if I could, but I'm not. But I was wrong to think you had a brain."

Karter leapt for Albert, but Lisa stepped in between the two angry boys.

She separated them and gave them each a stern look. "What's going on between you two?" she asked.

Albert and Karter didn't answer. A cool breeze brushed across her face, and she realized the second floor window was open. She looked out and could see a small crowd gathering below.

"You boys, stop fighting. This won't help us."

"You tell him that!" Karter screamed. "I'm getting out of her."

"To where?" Lisa asked.

"Anywhere but here." Karter stormed down the stairs, through the door and out to the front lawn. Albert followed him out of the house and into the street, with Lisa close behind.

"Just go. I will try to save Mom on my own. I don't need your help anyway. And as far as I'm concerned, you don't need to come back either."

"What are you saying?" Lisa asked Albert, confused by the blow up.

"Fine." Karter stormed off and disappeared into the crowd. "I didn't want to rescue her anyway. She doesn't deserve it."

"What was that all about?" Lisa asked. "We could use his help. You can't just let him go."

"He is a spoiled brat. He has been complaining since the day I met him."

"But tell me what started this. You two were getting along fine when I left you."

"I don't want to talk about it," Albert responded as he turned and walked back to the house.

Confused, Lisa followed. She wondered what they were going to do now. Everything was falling apart, and she felt like she was the only sane one left.

After the kids re-entered the house, the crowd started to disperse. A toothless, old man stepped from the shadows and brought a small microphone to his mouth. "This is Lucious, to Kos."

"Go ahead," Kos replied, crackle and static disguising his voice.

"It was smart to watch the house. It looks like that Mason guy is gone.The younger kid had a fight with the rest over not wanting to help save their Mom, and he has left the house. It's just the lion and the girl. What should I do?"

"Follow the boy that left," Kos said, chuckling. "If he is so against saving his Mom, let's ask him if he would like to become a Pirate."

CHAPTER EIGHT
FATHER AND SON

"Are you going to tell me what that was about?" Lisa asked, following Albert into his bedroom.

"No," Albert responded, coldly.

"Now is not the time for you two to be fighting; we have to save our Mother." Lisa stopped and thought about her statement. She had never been able to talk about her Mother in the present tense. Shaking away the unusual feeling, she stepped in front of Albert and stopped him. "What are we going to do?"

"We?" Albert responded, rolling his eyes. "*We* aren't going to do anything. Remember your lame promise. I am going to go rescue Mom."

"I want to help."

"What about the promise? I thought you couldn't break it?" Albert asked, sarcastically.

"With Karter and my Dad gone, I don't think there is much choice. So, I will ask you again, what are we going to do?"

"Well, when you put it that way." Albert smiled. "We are going to go see my Father. He wanted our help in finding Mom; well, I think we will need some of his help first."

"Are you kidding me?"

"Get your shoes on. I have a can stashed in the basement. I want to leave in a few minutes."

Albert and Lisa stretched out of the soda can in a bright beam of light. The warmth left their body and the two children found themselves in a set of trees just off the path leading to the Herionite castle.

"I hope you remember the phrase to get back," Lisa commented as the root beer can slowly stopped shaking. No matter how many times she traveled through the empty aluminum cans, it always amazed her how quick and painless the process was. It seemed so easy to be in different realms, different dimensions.

"Yes, I remember," Albert replied. "When you read the can, it's the fourth word from the left on the first line and second word from the right on the third line and then the first word after the ingredients."

"Just checking. So what do we do now? Walk up and knock on the door?"

"Exactly," Albert replied.

With Lisa close behind in shock, Albert walked up the front gate and stopped when two guards stepped in front of him. The upper half of the human body of the two guards began to shift, and within a few moments they had the upper bodies of wolves. Lisa stepped back and prepared to run, but Albert grabbed her by the wrist and pulled her closer. He wanted her to know she had nothing to fear. He could protect her.

"I am here to see my Father," Albert ordered, forcefully.

"He isn't available," the taller of the two guards

replied.

Albert called forth the lion from deep inside and growled without changing form. With wide eyes, the two guards took a step back. The loud sound coming from such a small boy was unnerving.

"You can either tell him I am here, or I can move you and tell him myself. Your choice."

The two guards exchanged looks of fear. They weren't sure what to fear worse, the King or his son. Either way they were in trouble.

"I will go get him," the taller guard said, realizing the son presented an immediate danger. He rushed into the gate and out of sight.

A few minutes passed and Albert was growing impatient. "We will go meet them." Albert announced walking past the guard.

The half-wolf, half-man didn't move to stop him. He understood that if Albert wanted to go in, he wasn't going to be able to hinder him.

"You are getting very bold," Lisa commented, scurrying behind him.

"You have to be, with these guys," Albert whispered. "They seem to only react when you scare them." Albert paused. "Look who we have here."

Rushing across the courtyard, a very haggard looking King John rushed behind the taller guard. His Captain of the Guard, Flug, was close behind. The puffiness around the King's eyes showed that Albert had interrupted a nap or a crying session of his Father. He doubted that King John, the Dark Red ever shed a tear, so he guessed his Father must have been asleep.

"How dare you come marching in here like this unannounced!" King John exclaimed as he got closer.

"This is not the proper way to announce yourself."

"Dad, do you want my help or not?" Albert asked, feeling Lisa's hand grabbing his. Her hand was cold and clammy. He could tell she was scared. He squeezed it for comfort.

"Of course," the King replied. "But whether you are in this castle or not, you need to learn the right way to do things."

"Whatever. Now that you have told me off, can we go discuss Mom?"

"Your Mother's condition is at the front of my mind. Let's go to the library."

Albert watched as his Father wiped a tear from the corner of his eye. He had been wrong; the King had been crying. But over what, his Mother? Could he really love her that much?

"What's up, Flug?" Albert said with a smirk, passing his Father's Guard Captain. Even after all the time they had been apart, he still felt a deep dislike for the cruel soldier. He often wondered if he hadn't made a mistake in not hurting Flug more severely during their first encounter.

Flug grumbled in response and followed along behind. He made sure to keep pace far enough back, so as to not be accused of eavesdropping on the conversation. He hated the boy with every fiber of his being. Patiently, he would wait for the chance to bring pain to the wayward Prince. This brought a smile to his face.

King John led Lisa and Albert into the castle, up a series of staircases and down a few short hallways.

Albert recognized the areas from places he had viewed from his time in the secret passage behind the walls. He tried to remember where each of the entrances and peepholes were. He wondered if the King had his men behind the secret areas watching people.

"In here," King John snapped, pushing the door open in front of him.

Albert and Lisa each took a seat around the long, rectangular table. The tall walls, full of books, cast various shadows across the slightly dark room. King John pulled open the curtains across a large window and chased the shadows away.

"Now, what exactly is it that you two need from me?" King John asked, motioning for Flug to take a seat at the table.

"Are you going to pay the ransom?" Albert asked, bluntly.

"Not if I can help it. I will try to delay as long as I can with as many excuses I can come up with. I do want your Mother back, but I can't let these terrorists get away with this. That's why I came to you."

"I just wanted to make sure whether this was about Mom, or the money."

"This is about your Mother. I just would prefer to save money if I can. And please show some respect. When you refer to her, do so as *Mother*."

"The child has never had any respect for anyone," Flug commented.

King John shot him a dirty look. He stared at his Captain and then turned back towards Albert. "As I was saying, please show some respect."

"If you want," Albert replied, casually. "What I need is to know is Mother's location." Albert stretched out the word, Mother's, sarcastically.

"The tracking device is in the tower," King John said, ignoring his son's sarcasm. "But I think you are familiar with that."

Albert smiled. He remembered how he had sneaked into the castle, used the device and escaped a year earlier. His Father had been furious.

"It's only good for a short time. They keep moving their location."

"I'm going after her right after this, so it should be helpful enough."

"Just you two?" King John was shocked.

"That's why you came to us," Lisa replied. "We can do this."

"Yes, but I thought you would enlist the help of your Father or the Realm Regal and the Coalition. Something beyond just you."

"The Realm Regal does not believe the Realm Pirates are back. They think this is some kind of trick you are pulling."

"That's ludicrous."

"If you hadn't spent so much time being deceiving to people, maybe they would have believed you. But they don't," Albert said, shrugging. "Let's just go find out where Mother is."

"Very well," King John said, walking towards the door. "You will come with me. I want your girlfriend to stay here with Flug."

"I am not his girlfriend!" Lisa yelled. She wanted to tell the evil man that they were brother and sister, but she stopped herself after realizing how much more trouble that would cause.

"Nevertheless. I want you to stay here." King John exited the room.

Prince Albert, Book 3: The Realm Pirates

"You better take good care of her," Albert said, pointing at Flug. "I would hate to have to come back here and embarrass you again."

Flug started to protest, but stopped. He watched Albert leave the room, turned back towards Lisa and smiled in a sinister fashion. It made Lisa uncomfortable; she began to count the moments until Albert would return.

"So," Lisa said. "You are the Captain of the Guards. That must be fun."

Flug grunted.

Without speaking, Albert followed his Father up to the cement courtyard on the upper tier of the castle. He remembered the area well. He had faced Flug and all of his Father's men, after tricking them into ingesting a white powder to suppress all of their beast forms.

"I understand you tricked Flug and my men up here a few years or so ago," King John commented, breaking the silence.

Albert took a double look at his Father. It was almost as if he read his mind.

"I needed your machine, and they were in my way," Albert responded.

"Even though we do not agree on your lifestyle, you should know that your actions and cunning were frustrating, but made me proud."

"I bet that was hard for you to say."

"Not at all; it is clear that you are a born leader and tactician. When this is over, I would ask that you reconsider your decision."

"Are you crazy? I wouldn't come back here for anything."

"Think about it. I am sure it would mean the world to your Mother."

"What about you?"

"It would not be completely unpleasant. Providing you could curb your tongue."

"I'll have to think about it later," Albert said, with a deep frown. "The last time I was here you tried to have me and Karter executed. That wasn't the best family memory I ever had."

"Agreed. But that was under different circumstances. Perhaps we will talk about it later."

Albert wasn't sure what to make of his Father's agreeing with him. Something seemed wrong. This whole visit was going too easy.

King John led his son across the courtyard and up the small staircase to the tracking room. Next to the entrance, a guard stepped forward and opened the door. Albert entered and the King followed.

The King stopped next to the guard and whispered, "Tell Flug to go ahead. He has about twenty minutes to secure the girl."

"Yes, Sire," the guard replied as he rushed from his post.

King John entered the tower and pulled the door shut behind him. The smile across his face was hard to hide.

CHAPTER NINE
FLUG AND LISA

Flug and Lisa sat quietly in the empty library; the sound of each of them breathing echoed through out the room. Periodically, Lisa would look up and quickly take a peek to make sure that the large, muscular man was not staring at her. Unknown to Lisa, Flug was doing the same thing. Occasionally, he would check to see if the blonde-haired girl was watching him.

"Captain Flug," a guard said, announcing his presence in the library. "I have a message that was supposed to be delivered to you."

"And what would that be?" Flug asked, pulling his long, black ponytail over his right shoulder.

"The message is, *go ahead, you have twenty minutes*," the guard whispered, looking toward Lisa and back to Flug again.

"Thank you, soldier. That will be all." Flug stood and walked around the table. The Captain of the Guards was smiling and unusually happy.

"What are you doing?" Lisa asked, pushing her chair back from the table.

"You might say, we are securing our insurance over the young Prince."

Flug moved quicker than Lisa anticipated a man of his size could. Before she could react, he was around the large table and next to her. He wrapped his large arms around her.

"Let me go!" Lisa exclaimed, kicking her leg back into Flug's shin.

Flug screamed out in pain and released his grip on the young girl. He stumbled back, holding his leg in pain. Frantic to protect herself, Lisa scanned the room for a weapon of some kind, but couldn't see anything to help her situation.

"You will pay for that!" Flug bellowed, recovering from the hard kick.

Lisa knew she didn't have much time. She moved to the closest bookshelf. Grabbing one book after another, she hurled them across the room at her attacker. Flug grunted in pain as about every other one connected with his forehead, but they didn't stop his progress. He maneuvered closer.

Lisa gave up on trying to fight and bolted for the door. She threw it open, but didn't rush out. Two guards, already transformed into their half-wolf forms stood ready for her. She stepped back into the room. Turning her attention to the large window, she was saddened when she saw that it was solid glass and didn't open. Lisa was trapped.

"King John and Albert are going to be very upset over this," Lisa stated, spinning to face the approaching Flug. "You'll be sorry."

"That may be true for Albert," Flug said, smiling. "But as far as the King goes, he is the one who ordered this."

"What?"

"You children think you are so smart. Did you ever stop to think that you only have a portion of the knowledge and experience that we do? Perhaps this will teach the arrogant Prince not to be so bold when he is in this castle."

"He won't help the King if you hurt me. You have to know that."

"It is his Mother," Flug laughed. "I think he will help. And if he doesn't, we will kill you. It's as simple as that." Flug drew back his fist and struck Lisa across the face.

Lisa's mind froze with black fear, and she lost consciousness.

Albert stared in awe at the gigantic device sitting in the center of the room. The smooth, blue, metallic look of its surface seemed out of place in the castle. It took up the entire floor space of the tiny area with the exception of a small, two-foot path cleared around the outside of its circular shape. The soft-green glow from the tracer's display screen cast an eerie, puke-colored shadow across all the walls.

"The sample is already loaded," King John said, stepping in front of the green-tinted console. "I will initiate the process, and we should have her location very shortly."

"Okay," Albert responded, making no attempt to further a conversation with his evil Father.

The tracking room was filled in silence and awkwardness for several minutes. The dead air was broken by the entrance door flying open and an out-of-breath guard rushing in. He took a moment to catch his breath and then stood to attention.

"Message has been delivered, Sire. The package has been secured," the guard reported between several heavy breaths.

"Excellent," King John replied. "You can return to your post now."

"As you wish." The guard bowed, exited, and gently closed the door behind him.

"What was that about?" Albert asked.

"That was something about an insurance policy that I had my men secure." King John motioned for Albert to join him on a set of two chairs positioned at an angle in the tiny rooms empty corner. "Please sit. We need to talk for a moment."

"This doesn't sound good. I think I will stand. What kind of insurance policy?"

"On you."

The King was being cryptic, and Albert was sure that he didn't like it. "What did you do?" A frown flowed across his face.

"I made sure that you get your Mother back, and that when you do, you don't try to convince her to leave me or to stay with you."

"What did you do?" Albert asked, concerned with the answer.

"I had Flug detain your little girlfriend for us."

Albert rushed towards the door. He had to save Lisa from that madman.

"You won't find her," King John casually said. "I have her hidden away."

"You'd be surprised what I can do. I will find her." Albert pulled open the door.

"I wouldn't do that if I were you." King John sat

smugly in his chair with his arms crossed. He stared at his son and waited for his reply. "It might not be too healthy for the girl."

Albert stopped and faced his Father. "And why is that?"

"If Flug hears you coming, he has orders to execute her."

"You really are a monster," Albert commented, through teeth clenched in anger. "And to think I was almost starting to like you. She had nothing to do with this. Why was that necessary? I had planned on doing this without any threats or kidnapping."

"Simply put, I don't trust you. I also thought it would be a good idea to show you that you are not as smart as you think you are. Consider it a hard, but good, lesson to learn."

Ding! Ding! Ding!

The gigantic device sitting in the center of the room began to vibrate.

"I believe we have a result," King John said, stepping in front of the panel. "Ah yes. They are still in the Amphibia Realm." The King read a few more lines of text. "It looks like they are almost 400 miles away from their last position. While you are gone, I will see if I can discern a pattern. If I see a trend I will get word to you."

"You are unbelievable." Albert was still in shock over the revelation. He had put Lisa in danger with his arrogance. What was he thinking by marching in here so boldly? This rescue was not just about his Mother anymore; it was also about his sister.

"I have had my men pack you a survival bag, and it is outside the door for you. I made sure you have food, water, rope, and a few other things. I would suggest you review it."

Albert didn't respond.

"You should get going," King John said, his voice calm and cold. "You wouldn't want anything to happen to your little friend."

"I'll go. But tell Flug, if she is hurt in any way, even a wood sliver in her finger, then I will hurt him ten times worse."

"I'll be sure to pass on your threat, Son. I'm sure he would appreciate it." King John smiled. "I don't know if you know this, but he doesn't like you very much. I certainly hope that the girl doesn't have to pay for his anger."

"And the threats keep coming. Well, here is a threat for you. When I get Mom and come back here, you and that long-haired monster of yours are going to be sorry. You can count on that." Albert exited the room and slammed the door behind him.

King John smiled sadistically. He was extremely pleased with himself and hopeful that his son would rescue the Queen.

CHAPTER TEN
PIRATES DISCOVERED

Mason hunched down behind the group of crates spread across the middle of the dock and watched the six Pirates walk past his hiding spot. Through a series of old contacts, he had managed to track the Pirate ship to one of the most overpopulated communities in the Amphibia Realm.

It was a smart move by the Pirates; no one would think to look for them in areas congested with people. No one, except Mason.

Fighting the urge to pounce on the unsuspecting Pirates, Mason waited patiently, making sure no other of their shipmates would come this way. A few moments passed; another group of five strutted by him and then another group and then yet another. He smiled. If he waited long enough, the entire crew would be in the city, and he could just slip on board the ship and rescue Nara. This was going to be easier than he thought.

Mason pulled a three-inch long cylinder from the inside pocket of his gray jacket. It looked like an ink pen, but heavier. He depressed a small button on the top of the device and watched for the soft, red light to illuminate. A second later, the red light appeared, and he tucked the device into the top of his right boot. No one would find it there if something went wrong and he was captured.

"How much time did the Captain say we had?" asked a toothless, dark-skinned Pirate, a few feet from Mason's position.

First Mate Kos turned to him and flashed his smile of missing teeth. "We have two hours to do whatever we want." Kos adjusted the strap on his eye patch. "But don't bring no extra attention to yourselves."

"Aye, aye," the Pirate responded, and he rushed to catch up to his friends.

Mason watched the scruffy-looking Pirate with the eye patch and wondered where he fell in the ship's command structure. From the conversation, he could tell he wasn't the Captain; yet the men took orders from him. It occurred to him that, if he captured this man, the one they called Kos, he might be able to use him as a bargaining chip to free the Queen. Mason scooted around the box and prepared to pounce on the unsuspecting man.

"Kos, Kos," yelled a young Pirate, barely old enough to have small amounts of hair growing on his face. The young man rushed down the dock and stopped a foot in front of the First Mate. He stood to attention and saluted his superior.

Mason wanted to hear the news. Silently, he moved back to his hiding position and watched as the scene unfolded before him.

"Enough of that," Kos said, waving the salute away with his hand. "What is so important?"

"We have him; we have him."

"Why do you always repeat yourself, Nicholas?

It is quite annoying."

"Sorry, Sir. But we have him."

"Who? Who do you have?"

"The boy we were following, the Herionite Prince."

Mason's ears perked up and he peered over the top of the wooden crate. The Herionite Prince? The man could only mean Albert or Karter. But which one?

"Really. Good work."

"We have him," Nicholas chanted.

"You already said that," Kos snapped. "Where is he now?"

"They are bringing him. I rushed ahead to tell you and the Captain."

"I will inform the Captain. The chain of command must be respected."

"Aye, Sir." Nicholas pointed down the dock. "Here they come now. We got him."

Kos shot Nicholas an angry look. Without saying a word, the young man knew what the glance meant. He apologized and scooted behind the First Mate.

Three Pirates marched proudly up to Kos. Between them was Karter. He had a small cut above his forehead. The First Mate looked down at the dark-haired boy and smiled. Mason wanted to leap out and save the boy, but if he was captured, neither Nara nor Karter would have a chance to be saved. He thought it was best to just watch.

"Congratulations on being the second captive from your family," Kos said, reaching out and patting Karter on the left shoulder.

"Captive?" Karter said, confusion in his voice. "I came to join you."

"Really," Kos replied. He cocked his head to the side and studied the boy. "Very clever. Join us, then you can escape with your Mother."

"It's not like that at all. Ask these guys." Karter waived to the Pirates next to him. "They can tell you what I was doing."

Kos looked to his men. The most muscular of the three Pirates nodded in agreement. "He's right, Sir. When we found him, he was asking how to join the Pirates. And when we captured him, he started rambling on about wanting to be one of us."

"That proves nothing," Kos said, directing his comment to Karter. "You could have been looking for a way to free your Mother."

"Well," Nicholas interjected. "When old Bill was watching him, he said this boy and the other kids had a fight. This here boy was screaming about not wanting to save his Mother and how much he hated the Herionites. I think he truly doesn't like them, and we are running low on men."

"Did I ask for your input?"

"No, Sir."

"Good. But whether you're on the level or not, you are just too young to be a Pirate."

Karter looked to his left and his eyes widened. He could see Mason looking over the crate at him. His guardian had heard everything.

"I'm willing to learn," Karter pleaded. "What if I gave you something to show you I'm telling the truth, something to, you know, prove my loyalty?"

Kos thought over the decision. What could the child have that he could possibly use? If it was useless, he could always just throw the child in the hold with his Mother anyway.

Mason watched in shock. What was Karter going to do? He wanted to pounce out and shut Karter up, but he couldn't do it without giving away his position. Why did Karter want to be a Pirate?

"What do you have that I could possibly want?" the First Mate asked.

"He's got nothing," the muscular Pirate said. "We searched him when we captured him."

"We got him," Nicholas repeated.

Kos grabbed the young Pirate by the hair, pulled him around and tossed him into the ocean. Nicholas flew through the air, screaming until he hit the water.

"When that idiot makes it back on the dock, toss him back into the water again. I want him to learn what happens when anyone irritates me."

"Aye, Sir."

Several more Pirates came down the dock to look at the captured Prince and to see why the First Mate had tossed the smallest of them into the water.

"Perhaps, if you had something to offer, I would be willing to let you start off as a cabin boy and work your way up." Kos said, turning his attention back to Karter. "I'm sure the Captain would approve."

"Your stupid sailor over there is right." Karter motioned to the muscular man. "I don't have anything on me. But what I do have is information. Something you might find very useful."

"I'm waiting."

"My Father is trying to figure out how to trick you and not pay you."

"We already know," Kos replied, not impressed

with the information. "That isn't anything we couldn't have figured out on our own."

"Well, how about that my guardian Mason is hunting for you guys?" Karter said.

"This is information I already have, too. We were watching your house. That is why we now have you. If you have nothing else then ..."

"Wait!" Karter screamed. "As I said, my guardian Mason is after you. But what you don't know, is that he is behind these crates."

Mason couldn't wait any longer and slipped his bag of gadgets over his back. Karter had betrayed him. Mentally signaling his beast transformation, his upper body began to distort. His upper body transformed into a fierce, blue tiger, including claws at the tips of the fingers on each hand. He would deal with the Pirates and find out what would possess the young boy to become a traitor.

Leaping from cover, Mason landed on the body of the closest Pirate to him. The surprised man didn't stand a chance. Mason struck out and sent the man spiraling off the side of the dock, five claw marks across his chest. Turning to the other Pirates, he paused. There were no longer just a few. Over twenty men had joined the First Mate and the betraying child.

"I wouldn't move," Kos said, drawing the sword strapped to his side. The Pirates around him all drew their swords in unison. "It appears we have you out-numbered and out-matched."

Mason looked at Karter and, between his sharp teeth, asked, "Why?"

"Simple," Karter replied. "You guys don't treat me nice and these guys will."

Prince Albert, Book 3: The Realm Pirates

"Do you know what you have done?"

"I think he does," Kos said, stepping in front of the boy. "He has just become a Pirate."

CHAPTER ELEVEN
THE CAPTIVE

With her eyes fluttering open, Lisa regained consciousness and surveyed her surroundings. She wasn't surprised to find that she had been brought to the castle's dungeon, but what did shock her was that they had hung her several feet off the ground by chains connected to her wrists. It reminded her of Albert's description of his treatment when he had been held here a short time ago.

"Ahh, I see you are awake," King John said, stepping in front of the dangling girl. "I trust that you are comfortable."

Typical of Lisa, she was not concerned about her current predicament, only worried about her half-brother. "Where is Albert?"

"He has left to rescue his Mother."

Lisa frowned. She hadn't expected him to rescue her, but it would have been nice if he had tried. She would have to find a way out herself.

"Don't look so disappointed," King John said, smirking. "He didn't have much choice. He wasn't going to be able to find you, and I told him that Flug would kill you if he tried."

Flug stepped forward from the shadows and

punched his left fist into his open right hand.

"He still may," the King added. "But for now, I ask that you just hang around and wait."

Flug let out a bellowing laugh that sent a chill up Lisa's spine. "That was a good one, Your Majesty. Very funny."

"Thank you, Flug. Now, come, we must discuss preparation in the event that my son fails. I will stop at nothing to get my wife back."

Flug followed the King from the room and soon Lisa found herself hanging in silence. After a moment, a soft whimper echoed from behind her. Twisting her bound hands, she managed to spin herself about 180 degrees. Hanging behind her, she viewed a small, crying man with red-shaded skin.

The whimpering creature wasn't human, or at least not human looking anyway. He had three large, bulging eyes centered on his face in a triangular shape around a small, pudgy nose and a large rectangular shaped mouth. Two six-inch long, white ears drooped to the side of his cylinder-shaped head, accenting the light-red tint across the creature's skin.

"Hello, my name is Lisa. What's yours?" Lisa asked, softly.

The red-skinned man slowly opened his eyes and focused on Lisa. He looked up at her hands and could see that she was bound the same as he was. Forcing a smile, he said, "My name is Duggie."

"Very nice to meet you."

Duggie nodded in agreement. "I, as well, but I wish it was in a more hospitable situation. Did I hear you mention Albert's name earlier?"

"Yes."

"Prince Albert Herionite?" Duggie asked.

"Yes, why?"

"I knew him for a short time. A very lively boy. I wanted to make sure he had got his sweater back that was left with me."

"The blue one?"

"Yes, that's it."

"He certainly did. He still wears it all the time. It's pretty ugly."

Duggie and Lisa laughed. Lisa looked up at her chains and back at the small man hanging next to her.

"What are you in for?" Lisa asked.

"I am the Royal Tailor. It is my job to clothe the King and Queen. We made a slight mistake in an alteration, and now we are being punished."

"What do you mean, *we*? I don't see anyone else. What did they do with the others." Lisa slowly swung back and forth to see if she was missing someone else in the darkness.

"You can't see them. I am a Hill Gnome from the Orange Hills of Ashburt in the Northern Province of this realm. My race is born as Quadads. We have three extra separate persons. I use each of them for a different part of tailoring. I, myself, take the measurements and control the other three with my orders. One of them, I use to write down the measurements, one is on the sewing machine and one does the hand stitching. They are invisible to you. They each have one of my eyes they use to see with, and I can use all three eyes."

"That's amazing!" Lisa exclaimed, her eyes wide with wonderment. "The things you could do with three invisible people."

77

"Yes, there are things that I do," the Royal Tailor responded. "I tailor."

"A lot of good that does you. It landed you here in prison."

"This wasn't the first time. Later today, I am sure they will let me return to work."

"What kind of mistake did you make to deserve a punishment like this?"

"It's kind of embarrassing."

"Please. I won't tell anyone."

"Very well," Duggie agreed. "I designed a new pair of trousers for the King. One of my measurements was slightly off and caused the pants to be tighter in the rear."

"That's all?" Lisa asked.

"Not exactly. The King was giving a speech to the market people and dropped one of his papers. He reached down to retrieve it, and his pants split all along his bottom. The crowd laughed at him, and it was humiliating for His Majesty. As a result, he has placed me here to learn from my mistakes."

"Have you learned anything?"

"Yes. I don't like hanging from my arms for long periods of time."

Lisa smiled and looked up at the chains around her own hands. The metal rings stretched high into the ceiling where they draped over a 'J' shaped hook.

"I think I can get us out of here," Lisa said, turning back to the tailor.

"I'm not going anywhere," Duggie responded, fear in his voice. "I am sure to be punished much more severely if I try to escape."

"Come with me. You don't have to stay here. No

one deserves to be treated like this."

"This is my job. I can't do anything else."

"Sure you can. You can do anything you want. You just need to try."

"No. This is what I was born to do. This is all I know. I don't want to leave this." Duggie shook his head from side to side. "Thank you for the offer, but I must stay."

"Are you sure?" Lisa couldn't believe that someone would voluntarily want to stay a captive. It burned at her from the inside. This sweet, short creature was a slave, who had been convinced he could be no better. But the words of her Father replayed in her head. She remembered how he told her that she couldn't make people change, no matter how right or wrong she thought they were. It was his choice.

"Yes," Duggie responded. "But I won't hinder you either. Try your escape; I will not tell anyone what you do."

"Okay, if you say so." Lisa mentally triggered the transformation into her beast form. Her upper body distorted and twisted, and feathers grew wildly across her chest and arms. The beak formed next as her face took shape of an eagle. Two wings sprouted from her back and developed into a large wingspan.

With a steady rhythmic flapping, her new wings carried her up towards the ceiling. The closer she rose towards the 'J' hook the more loosely the chain hung from her hands. She reached the hook, slipped it off the chain and let it fall to the floor.

Lisa gently lowered to the floor and undid the clasps around her wrists. Once free, she rubbed the raw burns left behind by the shackles. They hurt, but she didn't care; she was free.

"Good luck," Duggie said.

"I just don't feel right leaving you here. Are you sure I can't change your mind?" Lisa looked up at the dangling tailor.

"I'm sure."

Lisa nodded in agreement and made her way to the dungeon door. A small, barred window in the door allowed her to look out into the corridor and determine if it was empty. She scanned back and forth. Convinced it was clear, she opened the large iron door and slipped out of the dungeon.

With Lisa gone, Duggie closed his eyes and began to cry again.

King John and Flug sat around the small, white table in the corner of the Royal Chambers going over the movements of the Pirates. They were looking for a pattern or something to help predict their next stop.

"Sire! Sire!" a young guard screamed, rushing into the room.

King John stood, his face red with fury. "How dare you rush in here without knocking. Did I tell you to enter?"

"But, Sire."

"But nothing. Go back out and properly ask for permission to enter, and I will consider not sending you to the dungeon for a week."

"Yes, Sire. Thank you, Sire." The guard exited the chamber and pulled the door shut behind him. After a few seconds of silence, he knocked.

"Enter," the King ordered.

The young guard stepped in, shut the door behind him and stood erect in front of the monarch.

"Report," Flug yelled.

"The captive girl, the one who was hanging in the dungeon - she has escaped."

"She WHAT!" King John yelled, moving his face within an inch of the frightened soldier.

"During my rounds, I discovered her missing. The Tailor is still there, but ..."

"I don't care about the Tailor!" King John interrupted. "You should have told me the moment you entered the room that she was gone."

"But Sire, I tried. You made me go back outside and knock."

"Excuses! Flug, have this man executed after you have found the girl. I want this castle turned upside down. We can't lose her."

"Yes, Sire. It can't be that difficult to find one little girl." Flug passed by the King and grabbed the guard by his right ear. He led him out of the chambers and into the hall.

King John screamed in anger. His frustration was building, and once again it was because of a child. He felt the strong need to kill something. "Perhaps," he said out loud to himself. "Perhaps, I will have to conquer a new province."

Lisa crept down the hall, pressing flatly against the wall. She paid careful attention to check twice before proceeding around corners. Luckily, she remembered the secret passages that Albert had described to her. She was sure there were many ways in and out of the hidden area, but the only entrance she knew of was in the boys' room. All she had to do was make it there without being discovered.

The sound of rushing guards echoed from further up the hallway. They hadn't seen her yet, but that would change if she couldn't find a place to hide. She quickly tried to open the door closest to her, but it was locked. She went to the second and the third door. They were all secured and the guards were getting closer.

She knew her time was running out and her only chance was to keep trying the doors. One by one, she moved from door to door. Finally, she turned a handle and it opened. Lisa ducked in and feverously shut the door behind her. She leaned her back against the wood and listened safely as the stomping feet of the guards clamored by without detecting her presence.

To her relief, the room was completely empty except for a winding staircase that disappeared into the darkness above. Lisa knew the boys' room was near the top of the castle. She only hoped that the stairs would lead her that high.

CHAPTER TWELVE
THE BEAST MASTER

The large Minotaur stretched his arms high above his head as he yawned and fought back the sleep that threatened to overtake him. The huge horns of his bull-shaped head drooped along with his head as he crawled into his bed and turned off the light. He hadn't slept in almost twenty-four hours.

The children had been slipping into their beast comas a lot lately. As the Beast Master, it was his job to help them choose their beast faces and guide them on the path to enlightenment. What that really meant to him was his purpose was to make sure that they didn't screw anything up and hurt themselves. He had been doing the job for close to 1000 years. He loved it; it was just that, sometimes, it was very tiring. After a full night's sleep, he would be more positive about it. He was sure of it.

The sleep came upon him, and a dream seeped in with the gentleness of a soft white cloud. He was lying in a field of bright-purple grass. The sun was beginning to set and a cool breeze blew the small portion of hair hanging down between his two large horns. But as suddenly as it began, it ended. Like a puff of smoke, the images blew from his head and he opened his eyes to find himself back in his bedroom. What had just happened? How come he had awakened?

Knock! Knock! Knock!

The Minotaur recognized the sound. Someone was using his pig-shaped doorknocker to rap against the wood of his front door.

"Who in the heck would be coming at this time of night?" the Minotaur grumbled, looking at the clock on the end table. "It's the middle of the night."

Knock! Knock! Knock!

If he stayed in bed, maybe the visitor would take the hint and just go away. He wanted to ignore it, but each bang seemed to get more urgent and louder. Reluctantly, he climbed out of bed making no effort to cover his bare chest or raggedy sweat pants.

Knock! Knock! Knock!

"I'm coming," the Minotaur screamed, his voice tired and scratchy. "Hold your horses." He reached the door, undid the seven locks along the doorjamb and pulled it open.

"I need your help," Albert pleaded, not waiting for the half-asleep Beast Master to speak. The downpour of rain that had flooded the Beast Master's city for six days drenched his hair and clothes.

"You're soaking wet," the Beast Master said, concerned. "Get in here before you catch a cold." He ushered Albert through the door way and to the couch in the living room. "I'll be right back."

Albert shivered from the cold. He felt like his bones had frozen solid. The Beast Master reappeared with a dark-green blanket in his arms. He wrapped it around Albert and sat down in a small chair across from his friend.

"What brings you out on a night like this?" the Beast Master asked.

"I need your help."

"With what?"

"My Mom has been captured by the Realm Pirates, Lisa has been captured by my Father, and Mason is gone."

"Wow, you are having a bad day. But you didn't mention Karter. Where is he?"

"I don't want to talk about him," Albert snapped. "I just need to rescue my Mom and then on to Lisa."

"Tell me what happened."

Albert spent the next fifteen minutes bringing the large Minotaur up to speed on the events. He left out the part about the fight with Karter and being blackmailed by his Father. When he had finished, the Beast Master sat quiet with his mouth hung open. If he wasn't so scared, cold and frantic, Albert might have found his expression incredibly funny. But instead, he just restated what he had when he arrived.

"I need your help."

"And you have it," the Beast Master responded, patting the young boy on the shoulder. "The first order of business is to get a can transport to the Amphibia Realm. Let me get changed, and we will set out. You just stay here and keep warm."

Albert nodded in agreement.

CHAPTER THIRTEEN
STINK WORMS

The Beast Master led Albert down the darkened street of Uqwe City, the nearest town to the Minotaur's home. Dressed in large, oversized cloaks with brown hoods pulled down to cover their faces, they paid careful attention to stay dry beneath the overhangs and to keep their presence hidden.

Albert wasn't sure why the need for the secrecy, but the Beast Master had insisted on it - which meant they probably would be acquiring the enchanted soda can illegally. But he didn't care; he just wanted to save his Mother, and then Lisa.

"Here we are," the Beast Master whispered, cutting into the door of a shop. The sign in the front window read, *Stink Worm Dealer.*

"What is this place?" Albert asked, following him in. "Because on Earth, worms are ..." Albert gagged as the disgusting smell of the room filled his nostrils.

"I see from your reaction," the Beast Master responded, "that you understand why they are called Stink Worms. They have a bad natural odor."

"Why would someone sell this stuff?"

"You would be surprised in how many recipes

it's used. I admit it's an acquired taste, but the flavor is wonderful, depending on which realm produced the worm, especially if you eat it live. I fixed it once when you …"

"Stop right there," Albert interrupted. "Don't say any more, or I'm going to puke."

The Beast Master smiled and moved deeper into the store. He stopped at a small desk towards the back and rang the small, silver bell setting in the center of the counter. The sound of paper shuffling echoed from behind a curtain, and a second later, a man stepped onto the store floor.

"How may I help you?" the silver-skinned store owner said, picking a dark-colored substance from the corner of his light-blue beard.

"It's me, Tentric," the Beast Master said, pulling the hood off and revealing his identity. "I need to get a soda can to the Amphibia Realm as soon as possible, and no questions asked."

"Long time, no see, BM," Tentric responded. "But no questions asked, hmmm. Well, that's the trick, isn't it. And it's going to cost you. I need double the rate."

"Double!" Albert exclaimed, not even knowing the amount. He just could tell this shady, little man was trying to cheat them.

"That's fair." The Beast Master remained calm and cool. "But I need it within an hour."

"An hour?"

"An hour." The Beast Master stared intensely at the silver man.

"I will do my best, BM. I need to go make a few calls. Come back in an hour." The shop owner disappeared behind the curtain.

"He called you *BM*," Albert chuckled, smiling from ear to ear. "I know it stands for Beast Master, but in my realm it means ..."

"It means the same in this realm as well," the Beast Master interrupted. "It's not a favorite of mine, but it's easier to let him call me that, than fighting it."

"So, what are we going to do for an hour?"

"I need to wake up. There is a diner across the street. We can have something to eat and get a big cup of wirk."

"Wonderful," Albert said, sarcastically. "I hate the taste of wirk, and I'm sure Stink Worm is the only thing on their menu."

"As a matter of fact, they do specialize in worms, and wirk is good for you. The caffeine really helps; trust me."

"The last time someone told me that, I lost my beast form for a while."

The Beast Master stepped out of the shop and Albert followed. They ran across the rain-soaked street and quickly ducked into the diner.

"I thought we didn't want people knowing it was us?" Albert asked, shaking the water off his cloak and hanging it on a rack next to the door.

"Here it's fine. I just didn't want people seeing us go into the shop," the Beast Master responded, signaling a waitress from the other side of the room.

The waitress crossed the empty diner and stopped near the counter. "What can I do for you?" she asked, between loud chews of bubble gum.

"We would like a seat please."

"The place is completely empty," the waitress responded, rudely. "Sit where ever you want and tell me when you're ready."

"Excuse me," Albert said. "Does this place serve anything besides Stink Worms?"

"What do you think?" the waitress said, pointing at the sign that read 'The Stink Worm Diner' and then disappearing through the kitchen door.

The Beast Master led Albert to a booth near the front window. From their seats, they could see the Stink Worm Dealer shop across the street. Without a word, they each grabbed a menu and scanned for what they would want.

"Just great," Albert complained. "The only thing that isn't Stink Worm is fish, and I don't like fish."

"On page one, they have salads. Order one of those. As for me, I'm going to have a live, double Stink Worm burger."

Albert rolled his eyes as the Beast Master signaled the waitress. She slowly waddled over to the table and pulled a pad of paper out of a pocket in the apron she wore around her pink uniform. "What do you want?"

"I will take a salad," Albert ordered.

"What type of dressing?"

"Do you have thousand island?"

"Never heard of it. We have Stink Worm French, Stink Worm Ranch and Stink Worm Light."

Albert felt sick to his stomach. "I will just have it plain."

"Just lettuce?"

"Yes, unless that has Stink Worms on it as well."

"No, it doesn't." She wrote the order on her pad and turned to the Beast Master. "And you."

"I want a live, double Stink Worm burger."

Prince Albert, Book 3: The Realm Pirates

Albert felt sick. He thought about the shop across the street and all the jars of Stink Worms. He liked the Beast Master, but couldn't understand how anyone could like the foul smelling food.

An hour later, the Beast Master and Albert exited the diner and started across the street. The rain had stopped, and the streets were already beginning to dry. Several stars were shining through the parted clouds, brightening the area between the diner and Stink Worm dealer.

"I'm sorry I threw up on you, " Albert said, embarrassed by the event and holding his stomach. "I just couldn't watch you eat that. The way that worm wiggled through your teeth."

The Beast Master watched as Albert fought back the urge to throw up again. He patted his friend on the shoulder and smiled.

"It's alright," the Beast Master lied. He didn't want the boy to feel any worse than he already had. "At least you woke me up."

The two friends entered the Stink Worm shop, and as before, the smell assaulted Albert's senses and he had to fight the bile back down his throat. He didn't want to throw up again. He tried not to make eye contact with the glass jars swirling with Stink Worms.

"Do you want to just wait outside?" the Beast Master asked, concerned for his young friend. "I can do this myself."

"No," Albert responded, shaking the sickness from his brain. "I already made that mistake; I left Lisa alone and look what happened to her."

"Suit yourself."

The Beast Master rang the counter bell, and like before, the shop owner scurried out through the curtain. In his right hand he held an orange soda can.

"Here you go, BM," Tentric announced, proudly placing the can on the counter in front of the Minotaur. He held up an electronic pad to the Beast Master. "Your finger print for payment please."

Without question, the Beast Master placed his forefinger against the pad. The small device beeped twice, and the shop owner pulled it back to read. He watched numbers and symbols scroll down the screen. A moment passed and the store owner looked up and smiled.

"Payment has been confirmed. Nice doing business with you. If you ever have need of some Stink Worm patties or live Stink Worm noodles, don't hesitate to stop by. I will give you a great deal."

The Beast Master picked up the can and led Albert out of the store. Once in the fresh air, Albert took several large gulps and smiled when he could no longer smell the Stink Worms .

"I want to stop one more place and get some supplies, and then we are off," the Beast Master said, tucking the soda can inside his cloak.

Albert nodded.

"Don't worry," the Beast Master said, full of confidence. "We will get your Mother back, and no one will get hurt."

CHAPTER FOURTEEN
WELCOME ABOARD KARTER

Mason was dragged to the center of the ship and dropped at the ground in front of Captain Van Decken. He had been hit several times, and the beating had drained his energy, but he refused to be on the ground in front of a Pirate Captain. Summoning all of his energy, Mason climbed to his feet and met the Pirate eye to eye.

"Quite strong," Captain Van Decken said, impressed with the blue-skinned Mason. "I understand you are a transformer and can turn into a tiger."

"Ask your men to stand back, and I will show you first hand what my beast face can do," Mason grunted, between spats of pain.

Karter stepped out from behind the Captain and made eye contact with his former guardian. The two saw each other, and Karter could feel the anger in Mason's eyes bore right through him. Captain Van Decken noticed the exchange and took a step to the left, blocking the boy from looking at Mason.

"Oh, I am sure it's quite impressive, but I will have to pass ... I would like you to meet a friend of mine." The Captain motioned to the two-headed bird on his shoulder. "He is quite unusual."

Mason turned his attention to the odd bird and watched it change from blue to green. He looked at it, curious why the Pirate felt the need to mention it, and then turned back to the Captain. "So, you have an ugly bird. Big deal."

"Oh, he is quite more than that," the Captain said, chuckling. "Look closer at his two heads. Look at his eyes."

Mason took another glance and this time made eye contact with one of the heads. The eyes were an unusual mix of greens and blues. The colors seemed to swirl, separate, and then rejoin. It was interesting, but he didn't see what the big deal was. A moment later it hit him, a calmness he hadn't felt before. He started to feel his muscles relax and his brain became cloudy. The bird was hypnotizing him, and he knew it, but he was powerless to stop the creature.

Karter couldn't bear to watch the process. He knew he was supposed to be on the side of the Pirates, but something inside of him wanted to rush out and save Mason. But he knew he couldn't. The Pirates would surely imprison him, and it was too important that he be in good graces with the Pirates.

The bird left the Pirate Captain's shoulder and flew the short distance to Mason. It hovered in front of the face of the drowsy man, opening the lips of his blue mouth with its clawed feet. Mason's mouth fell open and drool began to drip down the corners. Inside his head, Mason tried to close his mouth, but the bird's hold was too tight over him.

"Do it," Captain Van Decken ordered.

The bird nodded and rested the tips of its two beaks on Mason's bottom lip. The heads inhaled a breath and spat a red liquid into its victim's mouth. Mason could feel the liquid drip down the back of his throat. It had no odor or flavor.

"Very good," the Captain commented, watching the bird fly back to his left shoulder. "Release him."

The bird flashed its eyes quickly four times and cawed. Mason was in control of his body again. He spat on the ground, but realized he had ingested all of the bird's spittle.

"You will find that you are a little different now." Captain Van Decken smiled, pleased with himself.

"What did you do to me?" Mason asked, wiping the drool from the corners of his mouth.

"Have you ever heard of Lupicine?"

"Of course. We use it in the Beast School to suppress the beasts. You can't transform if ....." Mason stopped as he realized what had happened. "That bird put Lupicine in my mouth?"

"Very similar. This bird is found in the jungle area that they harvest the Lupicine root. It has the same effect and doesn't have to be ground."

Mason leapt towards the Captain, but the Pirates were able to pull him back before his hands could reach him. He fought against them for a moment, but stopped when he realized how useless it was.

Karter felt a tear form in the corner of his eye. His guardian had been reduced and humiliated. He kept telling himself that he couldn't help. He had to be in good with the Captain.

"Take him below," the Captain ordered. "Place him in the cell with the Queen."

Karter's eyes lit up. The Queen? His Mother was

aboard the ship.

"Aye, aye," First Mate Kos responded, motioning for the men to bring Mason along.

"I hope your betrayal was worth it," Mason said as they dragged him by Karter.

Karter didn't speak. He watched as they roughly led him to the back of the deck and into the hold. Turning back to the Captain, he forced a smile to hide his extreme sadness.

"How do you feel about your former guardian being our prisoner?" Captain Van Decken asked.

"He was kind to me, so I am not too happy about it. But this is what I want my life to be, and if that means leaving everything I knew behind, then I guess I'm okay with that."

"Very good. You can be honest, but if you are to be a Pirate, you need to be ruthless. You have helped us greatly today with this capture. That is the first step on your growth."

Mason was led down the small staircase and through the ankle-deep water to a set of prison cells. He immediately could see an old man lying motionless in the one on his right and Queen Nara asleep on the bunk to his left. As the guards dragged him closer, Nara woke up and saw her first love coming her way.

"Oh, not you too!" Nara exclaimed, covering her mouth with her right hand.

The guards opened up the cage and threw Mason in. He tripped on the bar and fell face down into the water. Laughing, the Pirates re-locked the cage and disappeared up the steps and out onto the deck. Moments later, the hatch closed throwing the room back into almost blackness.

Using the light from several of the small holes leaking water, Nara helped Mason up and onto the bunk. He was soaking wet and began to shake. The coldness around was freezing him. Grabbing the blanket off of the cot, she wrapped it around him and snuggled close to him.

"Thank you," Mason said, feeling the heat of her body and the blanket warming him.

"What happened?" Nara asked.

"Actually," Mason formed a smile through the pain and cold. "I am here to rescue you."

She met his eyes, and they both started to laugh. Mason could feel the pain with each chuckle, but he didn't stop.

"You aren't doing a very good job so far. What went wrong?"

"Karter."

"Karter!" Nara exclaimed. "They captured him, too? Where is he?"

"He isn't a prisoner. He has joined the crew of this ship."

"Are you sure?" Queen Nara shook her head in disbelief.

"Yeah, pretty sure. He was the one that gave away my position and caused my capture and my subsequent beatings and power loss."

"That just doesn't make sense." Nara was confused by the behavior.

"I didn't understand it either, but I think there is something else going on."

"What do you mean?"

"He was trying too hard. He wanted them to know that he was trying to be one of them. And I overheard something that didn't make sense."

"What was that?"

"One of the Pirates said that he observed Karter and Albert screaming at each other. They were fighting over whether they should rescue you or not."

"What's so weird about that? Kids argue all of the time."

"Not Karter and Albert."

"They don't fight?"

"I didn't say that. They just don't argue. When they get upset with each other, they fight. I have seen them wrestle down a flight of stairs, push and shove each other, but never argue. They just don't do it."

"What do you think is going on?"

"If I was guessing, I would say that Albert has come up with another one of his plans. I just hope that this one works."

"Me, too." Queen Nara pulled Mason closer. It had been a long time since she had hugged the blue-skinned man. She had missed him. She wished she could go back to him, but she knew whether she stayed here or went back to King John, she would still be in a prison of sorts. Nara wished she were free.

CHAPTER FIFTEEN
THE AMPHIBIA REALM

Albert and the Beast Master exited from the orange soda can in flash of brilliant light. They materialized to their solid forms behind a pile of stacked crates and immediately examined their surroundings.

"It looks like the transfer went okay," the Beast Master said, comfortable that no one was watching them.

"Where are we?" Albert asked.

"We are in Adrienna, one of only four of the above water cities."

"*Above water*? You mean they have cities under water, too?"

"Oh, sure. This place is only ten percent land, and the rest is water. Most of the natural inhabitants are water breathers."

"That is so cool. Are we going to get to see one of them?"

"Doubtful." The Beast Master motioned for Albert to follow him out into the street. "The Pirates would need to dock to one of the four land masses for supplies and things. According to the coordinates from your Father, they are on the southern land mass."

"Then why did we come here?"

"You have been asking questions since the first time I met you. Don't you ever stop? Just trust me to get us where we need to be."

Albert smiled.

"Don't smile at me."

Albert smiled brighter.

"Ughh. Fine. So you want an explanation," the Beast Master said, faking frustration as he led Albert into the street. "This was the only place to enter the realm by a transport. We can get to the other land mass, but we need to acquire another means of transportation."

Albert followed the Beast Master down the street and into a market. It reminded Albert of the one outside his Father's castle, but with one big difference. These people seemed happy. They were selling fish, fruit and trinkets from their open tents with smiles and handshakes. It made him wonder if he could ever bring joy to his market like this, when he would eventually take over from his Dad.

"Are you with me?" the Beast Master asked, noticing Albert daydreaming.

Albert shook his head and put the thoughts away for another day. "Yeah. I'm here."

"Come on."

The Beast Master made his way through the crowd. Every so often someone would pat him on the back or tell him *hello*. He seemed to know quite a few people. This didn't make sense to Albert. If he knew people and was not hiding his appearance, why did they have to sneak into the realm? Something just didn't add up.

"I know you don't want to hear this," Albert said.

"But I have another question."

"Shhh," the Beast Master replied. "Wait until we are through the crowd."

The two friends made it through the crowd and ducked into an empty tent at the end of the row. The Beast Master stuck his head out of the tent to make sure no one had seen them. Once he was convinced, he ducked back in and addressed Albert. "What is it?"

"If you know everyone out there, why are we sneaking around? It doesn't make any sense."

"We are not just sneaking around. We are stealthily moving through to our destination."

"Same thing," Albert replied in frustration. "Why are we stealthily moving around? What do you have to hide?"

"You."

"Me? What do you mean?"

"I mean you. People know me. I have made a point for them to see and talk to me. As a result, they stay focused on me and ignore you. You get it?"

"I do, but why would they care about me? I'm just another kid to them."

"Ever since you mentioned to me seeing the man watching you at your house, I started thinking that they probably are waiting to see what you do. They will probably have people in the towns watching for threats to the Pirate ship. If all they see is me, then it will be harder for them to see you."

"Got it," Albert replied with a smile. "That's a good idea."

"Thanks." The Beast Master looked out of the tent again. "You wait here; I am going to get us a boat, and then I will come back for you."

Albert nodded in agreement and watched the Beast Master exit.

Almost an hour later, Albert was still waiting in the tent. He had almost given up hope and was considering going to look for his friend. He wasn't sure where to go, but it had to be better than sitting around waiting. To his relief, the curtain parted and his Minotaur friend returned.

"I have the boat, but we need to hurry. It appears that there is a skirmish beginning in the path we want to travel."

"A skirmish?"

"A fight, a mini-war."

"Ahh." Albert followed the Beast Master out of the tent.

The two companions made their way to the dock and down a flight of stairs to a rectangular wooden platform floating on the water. It alternately rose and sank violently with the rushing water. The odd looking boat next to it crashed against the wood.

At the bottom of the stairs a small-looking fellow dressed in a waterproof coat and boots met them. He smiled, stretching his gray-bearded face and motioned for them to enter the boat.

"You really need to be on your way," the boat merchant said, his voice scratchy.

Albert followed his motion and looked closely at the boat. It really wasn't a boat at all, but rather a mini-submarine, painted all in black with a large window across the front and three small, glass circles lined down both sides. It had one hatch on the top, and as he looked down the ladder, he could see three seats lined in a row from the front to the rear.

"I'm sure not going in there," Albert commented, stepping back from the sub.

"But we have to," the Beast Master replied. "There isn't anything else available."

"But it looks cramped, and I never did like the water much."

"If you want to rescue your Mother, you will get in," the merchant commented.

Albert looked at the Beast Master in shock. He couldn't believe that his friend had told the merchant about what they were trying to do. How could the Minotaur be so careless. Seeing the expression on his young friend's face, he understood immediately what the boy was thinking. "He's an old friend. I trust him."

The old man smiled. "Yeah, he trusts me, and so should you. Now get in."

Reluctantly, Albert climbed down the ladder into the mini-submarine. The interior was painted a bright yellow and reflected the two tiny, overhanging lamps, illuminating the small area.

The Beast Master followed next, but was stopped halfway in by the merchant . The older man shook his hand and went over the operating instructions for a second time with the Minotaur.

"Thanks, I think I got it, Joe" the Beast Master replied.

"Just remember to curve away from Neptunide. You need to give them a wide berth. King Trite has declared war on all air-breathing creatures, and the Mermen are enforcing his rule."

"I'll remember."

"And if you encounter any Mermen, don't try to reason with them. Just get away as quickly as you can. They have attacked five ships this last week, and each time they left no survivors."

"None."

"They're savages."

"Thank you old friend," the Beast Master replied, slipping down into the mini-sub. He pulled the hatch shut behind him and crawled to the front seat.

"Hey, watch it!" Albert cried, pushed to the inside of the hull by the Beast Master's large form passing him. "We don't have a lot of room in here."

The Beast Master took his seat and strapped his seat belt around his waist. Albert noticed that the Minotaur's huge form blocked the entire front window and forced him to only use the side glass for checking out the water.

"This is tighter than I thought," the Beast Master commented, scrunching down in the chair to keep his horns from scraping along the roof. The seat belt around his waist barely fit, and he was sure it was going to break. When it didn't, he smiled and turned back to Albert. "Are you strapped in and ready?"

"As ready as I'm going be."

"Here we go."

The Beast Master flipped on all of the control buttons. The console in front of him came alive with flickering lights and various beeps. It reminded the Minotaur of a small Christmas tree. If the situation wasn't so serious, he would have loved to take a few moments to watch the dashboard flicker.

Pushing the beautiful lights away from his

Prince Albert, Book 3: The Realm Pirates

thoughts, the instructions on how to operate the vessel scrolled through his mind. He recalled everything his friend had told him. Taking a deep breath, he grabbed the leather grips of the rectangular steering wheel between his legs and pushed forward.

Albert could feel the submarine slowly move forward and dip under the water. He watched the sunlight disappear as water bubbled up across his window and engulfed the tiny submarine.

The underwater craft lowered to cruising depth and turned to the south. Albert took a deep breath. They were close to rescuing his Mother. He just hoped that everything was in place.

CHAPTER SIXTEEN
THE OLD MAN IN THE CELL

Mason quickly sat up on the bunk, the effects of sleep fading away. He hadn't meant to drift off, but he guessed his body needed the rest. Nara was still next to him, her eyes closed and her head on his lap.

He felt renewed and full of energy. His body was quickly mending itself, and the strong pains he had felt earlier had become simple dull aches. The short rest was all that he had needed, and now he was ready to figure out an escape.

"Wake up," Mason said softly, gently kissing her forehead. He would have let Nara sleep, but now that he was feeling better, he would need her help to come up with a way out of the small cell.

"I must have drifted off," Nara replied, sitting up and stretching. "How long was I out?"

"Not sure. I fell asleep, too."

"You were out for a few hours. Now shut up and let an old man get some rest," an old crackly voice yelled from the other side of the hull. The Captain's old Father adjusted himself on his bunk and faced the couple.

"You can talk!" Nara said in shock. "Why didn't you ever answer me?"

"Didn't want to." the old man sat up, stretching his arms.

"This is the Captain's Father," Nara told Mason. "He keeps him locked up down here."

"What did you do to your son that was so bad?" Mason questioned, trying to make out the man's features through the darkness. "Maybe you can give me something we can use against him."

"What makes you think I did something?" the old man replied. "Maybe it was him doing something to me. Sometimes people don't like their Father, you know. Doesn't mean it was my fault."

"He wasn't trying to imply that it was," Nara interjected.

"But, oh yes, I was," Mason said, correcting the accommodating Queen.

"Leave me alone!" the old man yelled.

"If you want to get some sleep, you will answer my questions. Otherwise, I can talk all night."

"And he can do it, too." Nara added.

"Fine, what do you want to know?" The old man cleared his throat.

"I want to know why a man would lock his Father up in a cell."

"I didn't do anything," said the old man cracking the knuckles on his fingers. The popping of his fingers echoed in the tiny space. "He has been bad since birth. His whole life he has been treating people bad and hurting them. He was always fighting in school, never listening. It drove his Mother crazy."

"Children aren't born bad," Mason argued. "That is a learned behavior."

"It ain't anything I ever taught him. I hit him every

time he was bad around me. But nothing would work on his attitude."

"You hit him?" Mason shook his head in dismay. "That is a big problem. You shouldn't strike a child. That isn't the way to teach them."

"That was how I taught him."

"Then his Mother ..."

"In her letters, she never mentioned any reasons. I tell you he is just bad."

"In her letters?" Mason questioned. "Where were you during his childhood?"

"I traveled a lot. I didn't have much time to spend with him, with work and all."

"Did you ever see him?"

"Once a month or so I would stop by. He didn't need me; he was fine."

"Obviously not. No wonder he keeps you locked up down here. He is probably afraid you will run away from him again or hit him."

"Don't blame this on me. Children got to learn their own way."

"They have to be shown the way; then they can learn to grow." Mason threw his arms in the air in frustration. "I can't believe I am even having a discussion of parenting with you. I must be losing my mind."

"You were the one that brought it up. I just wanted to sleep, remember."

"Go to sleep, you old fool." Mason turned to Nara. "Why did I even talk to him?"

"Now you know how I have been feeling in the castle with that monster," Nara said, putting her hand on his shoulder. "I feel like my not being in the boys'

Prince Albert, Book 3: The Realm Pirates

or Lisa's life is the worst thing. I could easily become like that man over there."

"You?" Mason laughed out loud. "Doubtful. But me? I could see that. All those years that I dragged Lisa through my adventures with the Realm Regal, asking her to wait for things until I had the time, I've done what that old man did as well. I hope I haven't ruined Lisa."

"You've done a fine job, and when we get out of here, you can ask her. I am sure she will tell you the same thing."

"And what about you?" Mason asked. "Are you ready to be a part of their lives?"

Nara began to cry. She put her arms around Mason and kissed him on the lips.

"Yes," she said. "I will tell the Realm Regal that I am ready to come home."

"I might be able to help with that." Mason reached into his right boot and produced the three-inch long cylinder he had hid there before capture. He turned it to Nara.

"Is that what I think it is?" Nara asked, excited to see the device.

"Shhh," Mason cautioned. "Yes, it is. I activated the tracer just before they captured me. The red light flashing means that the signal is being received. We just need to wait for them to send help."

Queen Nara threw her arms around Mason and kissed him on the lips.

CHAPTER SEVENTEEN
KARTER THE PIRATE

Karter climbed up the rope ladder as quickly as he could. The wood in the rings deposited several splinters in his palms, but he didn't care. He had something to prove.

Below him, the entire crew of the Pirate ship had gathered for the initiation ritual. They cheered and booed as each side made bets on whether the young boy would succeed. But for Karter it wasn't about the money, he wanted to show Captain Van Decken that he was Pirate material and could fit in with the rest of the crew. He wanted the leader's full attention.

Reaching the top, Karter climbed into the crow's nest and rang the bell hanging overhead. The bell signaled the end of the test and sent a portion of the men below into cheers of congratulations as they collected their money from the ship's deck, while others cursed and screamed death threats to the exhausted boy.

"Wonderful job!" Captain Van Decken screamed, making sure Karter could hear him over the arguing Pirates. "I knew you would succeed."

Karter climbed down at a much slower pace.

His hands throbbed in pain, more severe than he had ever felt, but he wasn't going to show any weakness. These men had to believe he was capable of being a Pirate and every bit their equal in toughness and endurance.

"Well done," Captain Van Decken said, placing his arm around the surprised Karter. "I believe you have what it takes to move up."

"Thank you," Karter humbly responded. "I just do my best."

"Well, it is certainly much better than our recent additions."

The Pirate Captain pointed at Nicholas. The young Pirate looked up as he slowly pulled his index finger out of his nose. He made eye contact with the Captain and smiled. Realizing that the Captain had seen him pick his nose, Nicholas quickly moved his hand behind him and wiped his finger on the back of his pants.

"See what I mean," the Captain continued. "A real dullard. And some of the others aren't much better than him."

The Pirates all looked at Karter as if the comments from the Captain were his. The evil stares he received made the hair on the back of his neck stand up. These men wanted to hurt him. He had to do something.

"I have to say, Captain," Karter burst out loudly, "You have a fine group of men here. I could only hope to be half the Pirate they are."

Some of the looks lightened. But others saw it for what it was and intensified their angry looks of pain and hatred.

"Why, did you know that your First Mate, Kos, is an inspiration to me?" Karter continued.

First Mate Kos smiled and nodded as several of the Pirates patted him on the back.

"I am proud to be a part of the crew," Karter continued. "I hope that I don't make too many mistakes or anger these hard-working men."

Captain Van Decken smiled. He could see what the boy was doing. He had a strong survival instinct and would make an excellent Pirate. Although he wouldn't admit it in front of the other Pirates, the Captain saw a lot of himself in the young boy. Perhaps, this could be the chap to take as his son and raise him to take over the ship and his position.

"Kos," the Captain called out.

"Aye, Sir," Kos responded, making his way through the men.

"Why don't you come up with some tasks for our young friend here? Nothing too hard to start off with. I would be extremely upset if some harm was to come to him before he could reach his potential."

"Aye, Sir." Kos motioned for Karter to follow him. "Come on, boy; let's put you to work." Karter crossed the crowd and followed the First Mate to the front of the ship.

As soon as they were out of listening range from the Captain, Kos stopped Karter and said, "You don't fool me, boy. The Captain may have taken a liking to you, but I can see through that. If you step out of line, you can expect me to be there waiting to make you walk the plank. You understand?"

Karter swallowed hard, nodding in agreement.

CHAPTER EIGHTEEN
UNDER ATTACK

"What was that?" Albert screamed, pointing at the closest circle of glass to his left.

"Where?" the Beast Master asked. "I didn't see anything."

"It zoomed by us; look, there it is again." Albert pointed to the side window to the right.

A sudden rush of water passed by, leaving a wake of white bubbles. The water soon calmed, showing no evidence of the disruption.

"It's moving too fast; I can't see it. Maybe it will leave us alone," the Beast Master said, straining to look at the sea around them.

Albert undid his seat belt, stood and crawled to the front of the sub. He squeezed in next to the large Minotaur and stared out the front window with his friend. Studying the landscape and water around them, he scrutinized every bubble and movement of water, but couldn't see anything.

"I guess it's gone," Albert commented, turning to return to his seat.

"I don't think so," the Beast Master exclaimed, pointing out the front view port. "Look."

Albert followed his friend's motion. Directly in

front of them was a large sea animal that reminded Albert of a giant, green whale. It was moving towards them at a very quick pace.

"What's it doing?" Albert asked.

"It's not slowing down; I think it's going to ram us. Take your seat."

Albert rushed back to his seat as the sub turned on a right angle and headed out of the animal's path. He couldn't secure his belt around him in time, and the sudden movement of the tiny vehicle sent him crashing head first into the bulkhead.

"Owww!" Albert screamed, rubbing the red lump forming on his forehead.

"Sorry," the Beast Master called out. "You need to strap in."

Albert put the pain aside, crawled into the seat and pulled the restraining belt around him. Moments later, the tiny sub shook violently and turned on its side. It was still moving forward, just not upright. Albert found himself hanging sideways in the underwater craft, the belt holding him to the seat.

"What was that?" Albert asked.

"The whale thing rammed the back of us. I couldn't get completely out of its way. The left rudder is gone; I can't turn us upright."

"Do something!"

"I'm trying. Hold on."

The Beast Master pulled back on the control wheel and the sub started to rise. The whale-like creature came around for another pass and jammed its head into the bottom of the sub. The tiny vessel shook violently and spiraled away from the green sea creature, spinning in a clockwise circle.

"I think I'm going to be sick," Albert yelled out, covering his mouth.

The sea creature came at them again. The Minotaur had time to stop the spinning of the sub. He turned hard to the right and veered off as the whale zoomed by. Its attack missed the two friends by inches. Angry, the whale-looking monster turned back on the sub and swam at it again.

"Why does it want us?" Albert asked.

"It probably thinks we're food."

"What do you mean probably? If that thing breaks in here, we will be the cream center of his *submarine twinkee.*"

"What's a twinkee?"

"It's a tiny yellow cake with a … Oh never mind, just drive. Here he comes again." Albert held on tight to the grips attached to his seat and braced for impact.

The sea creature collided with the front of the sub. A loud creak and groan filled the enclosed space as a large crack formed down the center of the wide window. Small amounts of water started to leak in. One more hit and they were done for.

"Attention," a loud voice said through the ship's intercom. "You have entered Neptunide's restricted water-space. You are hereby ordered to turn around immediately, or our soldiers will respond with force. This will be the only warning."

"Oh, no!" the Beast Master screamed, fiddling with the controls. "How did we get so far off course?"

"Talk to them. Tell them what happened. They will understand"

"I don't know how to use the radio." The Beast

Brian Daffern

Master leaned down and pulled a book out from under the dashboard. "I'm sure it's here somewhere."

"You're reading the manual? I thought your friend showed you how this works."

"He did. I never thought I would have to use the radio." The Beast Master flipped through the book. "Ah, ha, there it is."

"Forget about the book! Here that thing comes again!" Albert yelled.

"Where?" the Beast master exclaimed, dropping the book on the control panel. A spark shot out of the dash and the sub dove deeper. The sea creature zoomed past them, missing the sub completely.

"Good one."

"Thanks," the Beast master replied, not sure of what he had actually done. Pushing a series of buttons, he leaned forward and spoke at the dash. "Hello, Neptunide. I ... I ... I got your message, but I can't turn back. We didn't know what we were doing. Soon as possible, we will turn around after we lose the thing chasing us."

There was no response across the radio.

"Do you think they heard us?" Albert asked, reaching for the book.

"I think so. I will try again. Hello, Neptunide. Do you hear me?"

There was a moment of silence ... and then suddenly the small sub rocked hard to the left. The scratching sound of metal against metal echoed through the tiny ship, hurting the ears of both passengers.

"That was different! Was it the whale again?" Albert asked.

"No, it was definitely something different." The

Prince Albert, Book 3: The Realm Pirates

Beast Master looked out of the window. "It almost sounded like a spear or bullet of some kind."

Both passengers peered out of the windows looking for the whale-like creature and whatever new threat was now outside their sub. The darkness of the sea surrounded them, and the faint light from the surface barely showed shapes in the underwater environment.

"There!" Albert exclaimed. "That whale thing is coming our way."

The Beast Master pushed to the left on the controls, but the sea creature adjusted its path to stay in front of them. Adjusting the pitch of the sub, the Minotaur turned the tiny ship over and headed in the opposite direction. He knew he couldn't outrun the monster, but maybe it would tire and leave them alone. But no such luck; it didn't stop coming.

The tiny sub approached a series of rock formations jutting up from the bottom of the seabed. Several small caves catacombed up and down the rock face. The Beast Master smiled; the tiny sub could fit in a number of them.

"I think I found us a good hiding spot," the Beast Master said, steering towards the closest of the tiny caves. "I just hope we can make it before that thing hits us again."

As if on request, the tiny ship rocked hard to the left, the same sound of metal on metal echoing throughout the sub. The Beast Master made a sharp turn and could finally see the culprit. Floating to their right were eight Mermen soldiers.

The lower half of their body was all-fish, fins and scales. The upper half was all-human. They had a face, chest and arms that looked the same as all humanoids. Across their bare, light-blue chests they wore straps with small metal balls secured across, and in each of their hands they held three pronged spears with gun barrels attached on the end. The weapon allowed them to stab or shoot. On a glance, Albert figured it was the metal balls in their straps that had been hitting the outside of the ship the last two times.

The Beast Master made another sharp turn to avoid the Mermen and directed the sideways-moving sub towards the cave. As the tiny ship moved forward, the Mermen were face to face with the approaching sea creature. They exclaimed in fear, bubbles frantically floating up from their gills and swam in eight different directions.

The whale creature didn't know which direction to turn. Confused, it ignored the Mermen and continued after the sub. The Mermen shot at the creature with their gun spears, causing the green whale to react as if in moderate pain. It turned back towards the sea men, but stopped when they dispersed into eight different directions again. The creature's small mind decided that they were too dangerous and instead continued on towards the helpless sub.

Thanks to the delay caused by the sea creature's confusion, the sub had plenty of time to make it to the caves. The Beast Master gently eased the tiny ship into a catacomb and backed into its black depth. The sea creature didn't slow its attack. It shot headfirst for the tiny cave. At the last moment it realized it could not fit into the hole holding the sub, but it was too late for it to turn back. Colliding with the rock face, the sea creature went limp. It had inadvertently knocked itself out. Slowly, it floated to the top of the ocean leaving Albert and the Beast Master in silence.

"That was close," Albert commented, breathing a sigh of relief. "Good job."

"Thanks," the Beast Master replied, taking a deep breath. "I hope we don't have to do that again. Next time you may have to go out there in your lion form and growl at it."

"Yeah, right."

Both passengers laughed for a brief moment. It was more of a nervous relief than anything particularly funny. They were glad to be alive.

"So, what's next?" Albert asked.

"I think we should give that thing a few more minutes to float higher. Then I will take us out, and we can make our way to the Province."

"What about those Mermen thingies?"

"They'll be back and probably in greater numbers. We will have to be gone by then."

The two friends sat in silence as minutes passed. They both studied the large crack in the front window and watched to see if it was getting worse. Albert figured he wouldn't worry about it if the Beast Master didn't. His friend would mention any danger.

"I am very glad you came along," Albert said. "I really don't think I could have done this without your help."

The Beast Master started to blush. He didn't take compliments well. He swallowed hard, and said, "You're welcome. It was an honor to be asked."

Both smiled at each other.

"Okay," the Beast Master said, breaking the

awkward silence. "Let's get going. We have a pirate to visit and a rescue to mount."

The Beast Master moved the sub out of its hiding place. He did so slowly, scanning the area for any possible dangers. Once sure they were safe, he pushed on the controls, and they continued on their side towards their destination. The feeling of being on their side was odd, but again, they were just happy to be alive.

CHAPTER NINETEEN
THE COALITION FORCE

Admiral Nakita straightened his dark-blue uniform and sat down at the small, round table. His normally light-orange skin was darkened in the cheeks as he fought to catch his breath. He hadn't stopped moving since he received the urgent communication from the Realm Regal's assistant. There were citizens to protect. But if the Realm Pirates were really back, he wondered whether even his Navy would make anyone safe.

"Thank you for coming, Admiral," the Realm Regal said, stepping into the room from a side door. "I have Captain Antilles waiting on screen. Video!"

A large panel slid to the side and a thin view screen lowered from the roof. It stopped a few inches above the table and turned itself on. The ruffled image of Captain John Antilles filled the screen. The strong wind blew his long, blue hair wildly about his head. He made no attempt to control it. He accepted it and listened intently to what the Regal had to say.

"I am assuming that my message was relayed correctly. The Realm Pirates are back," the Realm Regal said, sitting down at the table.

The two men nodded in agreement. The Realm

Regal could tell by their expressions they were deeply disturbed by the news. She didn't want to give them a chance to be frightened; she needed them focused.

"But we don't have any confirmations on the size of their force. It appears that a single ship kidnapped one of our agents."

"One of ours?" Admiral Nakita replied, his voice deep and hollow sounding.

"Yes. They have kidnapped Queen Nara of the Herionite realm."

"Not Nara!" Captain Antilles said, shaking his head in disgust. "She had provided us vital information. It will be a loss with her gone."

"We don't know that she is gone yet," the Realm Regal said, quick to make it clear. "What I want to do is mount a rescue mission."

"Those Pirates don't take prisoners," the Admiral said, wiping sweat from his upper brow.

"It appears they have asked King John for a large ransom."

"Not their old ways, but it could be to our benefit. Do we know if he will pay it?"

"Not sure. But Mason seemed to think that he wouldn't, but I don't know."

"I can gather our ships and we can attack," Admiral Nakita said, pushing his chest out. "We will not let them defile this office again."

"Calm down, Admiral. I, for one, do relish the opportunity to avenge my Mother," the Realm Regal replied, flashing her beautiful, perfect smile. "But we aren't even sure where they are right now. We have a general idea, but no confirmation. That's where you come in, Captain Antilles. We think they may be in your area."

Captain Antilles froze. The glaze across his eyes became shiny, and he made no attempt to hide the fear washing over him. Quickly, he got control of his emotions and nodded.

"We haven't seen any reports, but we will keep our eyes open."

"You mentioned that Mason didn't think the King would pay. If I know him as well as I believe I do, he is going to do something about this," Admiral Nakita said. "Remember how crazy he got when Lisa disappeared. How is he handling this?"

"I thought so as well. I asked him not to get involved, but when I sent a messenger to his house to invite him to this meeting, he was gone."

"What did Lisa say?"

"She was gone as well. As a matter of fact, so were Albert and Karter."

"He wouldn't take them all on this fool's errand. Maybe they …"

"No, they're gone," the Realm Regal interrupted. "Their house has been empty all day. I'm sure he will turn up, and when he does, he and I will have a little talk."

"If I see him on my patrol, I'll let him know you wish to speak with him," Captain Antilles said, clearing his throat.

The door to the meeting room opened up and the Regal's yellow-skinned assistant bolted to her side. He whispered several things into her ear and stood up. The Realm Regal turned back to the screen.

"It appears we have received a tracing signal from Mason. At least a device with his signature," the Regal said. "I am going to put you on a split screen,

Captain."

She pushed several buttons on her desk and the image of Captain Antilles squeezed thinner and moved to the left. An image to the right appeared with twelve circles, each with the name of the realm above them. A red dot flashed next to the realm with the Amphibia name. The Realm Regal pushed another button, and the image zoomed in on the Amphibia realm. The oceans flowed across the entire screen.

"You can't see this Captain," the Admiral said, leaning towards the screen. "But it is zooming in on the Northern Province."

"Not a good area," Captain Antilles said.

The picture on the screen continued to adjust and finally stopped at a patch of water miles off the shore from the nearest land. Slowly the dot moved across the screen in a southern heading.

"The signal is heading away from you, Captain," the Admiral said. "What is your best speed with the weather conditions?"

"In the air? My ships can overtake their position as long as they are sailing and not flying."

"The speed their dot on the screen is moving doesn't seem to very fast," the Admiral said.

"We don't even know if he is with the Pirates. This could be something else entirely." The Regal pointed at the screen.

"It's worth investigating," Captain Antilles replied. "Mason deserves that much."

"I would concur," the Admiral replied. "I will recall all personnel and get our ships ready. If Captain Antilles finds something, we can be ready to box them in."

Prince Albert, Book 3: The Realm Pirates

"I want to approach this situation with caution, gentlemen. I don't want to get our people killed. I want to remind you that we don't even know if the Pirates are back or if this is some kind of trap."

"Agreed," Captain Antilles said. "I will sign out now. I have to prepare to get under way."

"Good luck, Captain."

The left side of the screen went blank. The Realm Regal shut off the map and pushed a button to retract the screen.

"I want to be clear on this Admiral. If it is the Realm Pirates, I want their ships *destroyed*. They cannot be allowed to grow."

"Complete destruction? That hasn't been our way. Should we not capture them and imprison them?"

"No, they need to be *destroyed*, and I will hear no more of this."

"Regal..."

"No more."

"Yes, Ma'am. But Regal, there is a part of this that is bugging me. I thought we already destroyed all of them twenty years ago. Where have they been hiding?"

"That's a very good question," the Realm Regal said, standing. "But I want to address your first part. These terrorists will be *destroyed*. There will be no argument. Do you understand me?"

The Admiral nodded in agreement.

"Good."

CHAPTER TWENTY
MISSED

"Are we there yet?" Albert asked, stretching his arms out in front of him during a wide yawn.

"It's only been ten minutes since you asked me last time," the Beast Master grunted. "And I will tell you what I told you before; we are still a few hours away. Try to relax."

"I can't. After being chased by a giant sea creature and attacked by Mermen, it just seems dull. And I can't stop thinking about my Mom. I hope that they haven't hurt her."

"I'm sure she is fine. If you want to worry about something, worry about the large crack down the center of the front window."

Albert looked beyond the Beast Master and could see the water slowly leaking through the crack formed from the whale-like creature colliding with them. He had almost forgotten about the damage to the little sub. His mind filled with dread over the possibility of them drowning. He became completely quiet.

"That's better," the Beast Master said, smiling to himself.

The sub propelled along in silence for several more minutes. The Beast Master kept it close to the surface, but far enough down not to be seen from above the water. He didn't want to be detected.

"Beast Master?"

"Yes, Albert."

"How long until we get there? I think I have to use the bathroom."

"You have got to be kidding. You haven't had anything to eat or drink."

"Hey, you can't control this kind of thing. I need to go."

Before the Beast Master could answer, a loud, beeping alarm echoed from the dash, as it flashed red lights. The Minotaur quickly scanned the console and shut off the sound with a flip of the toggle switch.

"What was that?" Albert asked.

"Proximity warning. There is something big above us. Hold on."

"It's not the whale again, is it?"

"Not on the surface."

The Beast Master angled the tiny ship down, and the large boat passed over them. Once they were clear, he drove the sub up to the surface and studied the ship that was sailing on.

"That's them," Albert exclaimed. "Look at the black flag."

Hanging from the large center mast, the black, skull-and-cross-bones flag fluttered in the wind. It taunted the two companions, daring them to try to catch the mighty ship.

The Beast Master throttled the sub forward and dipped it under the water. He followed the large vessel, but found they were quickly falling behind. Even if the sub hadn't been damaged, he doubted he would have been able to catch the sailing vessel.

"You're going to lose them!" Albert exclaimed, moving up next to the Beast Master.

"I'm trying. With all of our damage, they are too fast for us. Now get back in your seat."

"I don't want to. You have to do something."

"I'm going to keep following them, but if you have an idea, I would be happy to hear it."

Albert shut up and just continued to dance nervously next to his friend. He could see the ship get further and further ahead of them. Suddenly, a bright flash filled the water.

"What is that?" Albert asked.

"They are opening a portal. They are leaving this realm."

"Can we follow them?"

"Most of the big ships have those portal crossing devices, but this machine is too small. It doesn't have that capability. But if I can edge us close enough, we can follow them through it."

The Beast Master brought the ship above the water and pushed on the accelerator with all of his strength. The large Pirate ship began to disappear into the light. At first it seemed that the ship had been stretched twice its length, but it was an optical illusion as the form became light and disappeared in the portal.

"It's starting to close!" Albert screamed, pointing to the shrinking portal.

The tiny sub surged on, its small engines starting to smoke. The portal was slightly bigger than the boat, but they were still too far away. It shrank more and more. Albert could see they were not going to fit. The Pirates were going to escape. At the last moment before the brilliant light closed in on itself, a large bottle flew through the portal and bounced off the front of the sub's window. The crack widened slightly, but the bottle didn't break.

"Did you see that?" the Beast Master asked. "They threw their trash at us."

"I don't think so," Albert replied. "Unscrew the top, and let me climb out."

"Are you crazy?"

"I need to retrieve that bottle before it sinks. Please."

The Beast Master released the door from his console, and the wheel on the entrance unlocked. Albert spun the circular wheel to the left and pushed on the top. A loud, hissing sound rang out as the air seal released the stale air from the sub

Albert climbed out on the front of the sub. The cool ocean wind blew on him like a fierce gale. Holding onto a hand grip, he eased himself closer to the water. He marveled at all the dents and scrapes across the hull of their small vessel. Between the Mermen and the sea creature, they were lucky the sub was still in one piece.

Turning his attention to the ocean, Albert scanned the water and could see the bottle floating a few feet away. He stretched for it, but it was just out of his reach. He scooted down further on the sub and reached, but once again, he couldn't get it.

Taking a deep breath, he jumped off the ship and swam towards the bottle. The temperature of the water was so cold he could feel the hair on his arms stand up, and his skin turned bright red. Pushing the freezing cold from his mind, he made his way to the bottle. He gripped it in his right hand and swam back by kicking and paddling with his left hand. Albert climbed back on the sub, balanced himself and then crashed the bottle against the side.

"What are you doing?" the Beast Master asked from within.

"I'll be there in a second," Albert responded, digging through the pieces of broken glass. He picked out a small, white paper. He opened it up and read it. "There you are."

He tucked the paper into his pocket and climbed back down the ladder. He secured the door behind him and took his seat.

"So, what did you find out there?" the Beast Master asked.

"A little help," Albert said, shivering so hard his teeth chattered. "Is there anywhere, in that land mass we were headed towards, to get a transport soda can."

"Definitely not into this realm, but maybe, on the red market we can find one out of the realm. Why do you ask?"

"We need to get to the Martery Realm. That's where the Pirates went."

"How do you know that?"

Albert smiled. "I just do."

Lisa was beginning to give up. The staircase she found had led her to more similar looking passages. She had been wandering through the tunnels for more hours than she could count. Through the tiny holes in the walls and the eyes of various pictures, she could see guards and servants go to bed and wake again. She wondered how much time had passed and how much more time would have to go by before she could find a way out.

Exhausted, Lisa slid down the wall and sat on a dirty floor. She heard the sounds of guards rushing by on the public side of the barrier, and she turned to look out the tiny holes. A smile spread across her face. She recognized the hallway. King John and Flug had led her and Albert there for the meeting.

Lisa recalled her memory of the path they took and determined that, if she went several more feet down the left tunnel, it should lead to an area just outside the doorway. And once she was there, she could sprout wings and fly freely away.

"Alright," she whispered, discovering a new-found energy.

Jumping to her feet, Lisa sped down the passageway and stopped as it dead-ended at a man-made, stone wall. She peeked out the nearest hole and could see the doorway on the public side she needed to pass through. But how was she to get out of the tunnel?

Feeling across the wall, she searched for a latch or release that would open a doorway. Albert had told her they were all over the passageways; she just needed to find it.

Within a few moments, a loud click went off, and a portion of the wall swung open. She found the opening latch. Cautiously, she stepped out and looked both ways. The coast was clear. Not taking the time to close the wall, she bolted directly for the doorway. Suddenly, she found herself standing in the warmth of the morning sun. Its bright rays bombarded her skin. She had been in the dark so long, it took her eyes a few moments to adjust. But once they did, she wished they hadn't. From across the pavement, several of the Herionite guards rushed towards her, and they didn't look happy.

Signaling her transformation, Lisa's upper body began to twist and distort until she found herself with a beak and large flowing wings. Flapping them continuously, she slowly rose off the ground and out of the reach of the frustrated men.

"Good bye, boys!" Lisa exclaimed, flying farther into the air. "Thanks for the stay. Hope not to see you too soon."

A large arrow flashed by her head, barely missing her neck. Somebody was shooting at her, and they had almost got her. Lisa flapped in place and looked back in the direction of the shot.

Standing on one of the elevated towers, the Captain of the Guards, Flug, and two of his men were holding bows. They each loaded an arrow and released it into the air. The first two missed wide, but the third one scratched her left arm.

Lisa turned and flew with all of her speed. She rose and dove hoping to avoid the onslaught of wooden sticks. The arrows kept coming and their aim was getting better. Given enough time, she was sure they could hit her. Climbing higher into the air, Lisa turned and dove for the front gate. Her speed continued to build. The arrows couldn't keep up with her and all the rest swished through the air a safe distance away.

Lisa glanced to her left and could see Flug screaming in frustration. Albert had been right, it was fun to see the Captain mad. But even angry, she was sure Flug was still dangerous. She was surprised when she saw him reach for another arrow. He pulled back and fired into the air. The stick passed close by her, tearing a portion of her pants, but not drawing blood. If she had been any closer to him, it would have been deadly. But now she was just too far away for his aim to be perfect.

Without further incident, she cleared the top of the castle wall and felt safe. The cut on her left arm was still hurting, but the bleeding had stopped. She was free. Now she just needed to figure out how to find Albert and how to help him rescue their Mother.

CHAPTER TWENTY-ONE
CAPTAIN VAN DECKEN

With his ankles and wrists bound by heavy chains, Mason was led from the dark cell into the bright sunlight, washing over the deck. His eyes began to water, and it took a minute for them to adjust to the brightness. He could see blurry images of the crew standing around him and the Captain leaning against the center mast. They had left Nara in the cell, which made Mason wonder what they were going to do with him.

"Ah, here is our guest now," Captain Van Decken said, a large smile across his face. "I trust that you are happy with your room."

"Sure," Mason replied - his lips cracked and bleeding from lack of drinking water. His stomach growled from hunger, but he wasn't going to show weakness to this group of terrorists. "I just wish the crew didn't smell like sewage."

The Pirates started to laugh but slowly stopped as, one by one, they realized the prisoner had just insulted them. Immediately on understanding this, their faces transformed into angry scowls.

"You can't talk to us like that," Nicholas yelled, stepping between two of the more senior Pirates. "We be Pirates!"

"And so well put," Mason responded, quickly. "So, the boy has to step up and speak for this motley crew. He must be the bravest of you all."

Several punches flew through the air connecting with the side of Mason's head and body. They came so quickly, he didn't have the time to dodge them. Each blow hurt worse than its predecessor, and he found it difficult to remain standing. The twelfth fist that connected with his head was all he could take, and his legs buckled beneath him. He fell to the ground with a loud thud, banking his head on the hard wooden deck.

Karter watched the attack from high atop the mast in the crow's nest. He wanted to rush down and help his guardian, but he just couldn't. He hoped Mason would understand, but from the rough treatment and blood flowing from an open cut on his forehead, he didn't think Mason's chances were good.

"Get our guest back on his feet," the Pirate Captain ordered, stepping forward.

"It takes a mighty big man to hit someone that's tied up and outnumbered," Mason said, climbing to his feet. "Did you ever just go down, yourself, and beat on your Father, or did you send one of your men to do it?"

Several Pirates rushed towards him, their hands high into the air.

"Hold," the Captain ordered. "We're not savages. The man is entitled to his opinion. Besides, we won't find out any information if you knock him unconscious. Will we?"

"What kind of information?" Mason asked.

"In due time. I will give you a chance to tell us everything in just a few minutes. But first I need to know something about the year we are in."

"The year? I think you've been playing Pirate too long. It's the same year it was last month and the month before that."

"Well, that's good and all, but we were not in this year last month."

"I won't fall for any of your tricks," Mason said, confused by their ruse.

"I assure you it is no trick. Fifteen days ago it was some twenty years ago. We sailed through a vortex with our three other ships, and *boom*, we are twenty years into the future. A soft future I might add."

Mason wasn't sure he could believe them. He had heard of a few incidents of time travel, but nothing as big as a ship, or four ships in this case. But it would explain why this Pirate ship suddenly appeared. What if they were from the past?

"We were locked in a battle near the coast of the Webnock Capital. The Regal's forces had us pinned down, and then Kos sold me on the idea of using a device we captured on a raid."

"Another reason why the Webnock Realm hates pure humans."

"They were very trusting, but nevertheless, we took what we wanted. We always take what we want; it's our way. So we hooked up the device to the ship, and we found ourselves here, twenty years later."

"And you wasted no time in dropping into your old ways."

"Technically it isn't our *old* ways. To us it was just yesterday. But when I put my spies out into all the communities, I was able to launch this kidnap plot and understand a way to make a lot of money. But, all of that said, none of my spies have been able to gather what happened to the People's Association of Piracy. Our brothers seem to be gone."

"They are. After the death of the Realm Regal, the forces searched out and destroyed every last ship and Pirate. Until your appearance, the Coalition thought it had been successful."

"The Coalition was wrong."

"Yeah, I guess so. But even if you have four ships, it won't be long before you are forced to surrender to us again."

"*Surrender?*" Captain Van Decken asked. "You mean *be annihilated* like what you did to the rest of my people. There is no honor in extinction."

"That was a different time. We were different people. Do I want to hurt you? Yes. But do I want you dead? Absolutely not. Peace is the answer, not murder."

"You mean war."

"War, murder, it's the same thing when humans are forced to kill each other."

"Did you fight in the war?

"Yes, I did," Mason replied. "I was younger and did not have the same views I do today. In retrospect, the war was wrong."

"Bravely put. But your pacifist attitude isn't going to help you. It is time for you to give me that information you were so eager to deny me before."

"I don't have any information."

"I want to know about the Realm Regal's forces. How far away they are? How many ships does she have? And what is their attack plan?"

"I came alone. There is no plan, there is no rescue, and I am not in the Navy, so the number of ships isn't something I know."

Captain Van Decken stared at his blue- skinned captive. He studied his face and looked for any sign that he was lying. Knowing this, Mason raised the corners of his lips in a smile.

"That's all the information I know."

"We will see about that?"

The old man shifted on his mattress and sat up. He looked across the dimly lit hold and could see Queen Nara crying. Brushing away the sad image, he rolled over and brought his pillow above his head. The soft whimpers of her sobs echoed through his head. He couldn't stand it anymore.

"What are you crying about?" the angry old man asked, sitting back up.

"Aren't you listening?" Nara answered, wiping the wetness from her cheeks. "They were hitting him and torturing him. He's a good man, and he doesn't deserve this."

"Well, I'm sure you're right, but don't worry none bout him. They will rough him up a little bit, but he won't be killed or nothing. My boy likes to play bad, but murder isn't his game."

"You will have to excuse me if I don't share your optimistic appraisal of the situation. Look at how he has treated you."

"Yeah." The old man nodded in agreement. "But I wasn't completely honest earlier. I wasn't always a good man. I might deserve this."

"What did you do?"

"I used to be Captain of this boat before the war. I was not the nicest to the ships I came across, and I did some looting and kidnapping. His Mother was one of them I kidnapped. I took her from her life and made her my wife. My son was born a year later. He hasn't forgiven me for this life."

"He hasn't fought to get out of it either. He seems to enjoy it."

"That'd be true. But still a part of him wants to blame someone, and I am the easiest. I guess it's easy for me too. I could have escaped a few times, but each chance I had something made me stop. It was almost like a part of me wanted to stay here."

"Do you know a way out of here? If you do, tell me. I can go help him." Nara pointed to the top of the ship.

"It's suicide. You wouldn't get very far. And even if you rescued him, where would you go? There is nothing but water around you."

"I will figure that out when the time comes. Tell me. Is there a way?"

"Yes, there is a way. But if I tell you, you have to promise me that you will not tell my son you got it from me."

"Agreed."

"Okay, I'll hold you to that. Now, here is what you are going to do."

CHAPTER TWENTY-TWO
THE MARTERY REALM

The root beer can opened up, and the light forms of Albert and the Beast Master streaked out to the soft sand of the beach. Albert recalled his last trip to the Martery Realm and shivered as he remembered the large crabs and the events with Mr. Papaclock. He looked up to the large Minotaur and thought about sharing his sick feeling, but decided it was better to stay focused on the hunt for the Pirate ship.

"You've been here before, haven't you?" the Beast Master asked.

"Yes. When we had to rescue Lisa," Albert replied, reluctant to get distracted by the conversation. He had told the Beast Master only some of the details of their trip here, but neglected to talk about his captivity and his brother sending the evil teacher to almost certain death. He wanted to keep that inside. "But let's talk about it later."

"Look!" the Beast Master exclaimed, pointing down the beach. "Isn't that the Pirate ship?"

Albert studied the design closely. Even though there was a black flag flying high above, it was not the same ship. A sinking feeling erupted in his stomach; there was more than one Pirate ship.

Prince Albert, Book 3: The Realm Pirates

"That's not the same ship, but maybe they can lead us to the others," Albert replied, starting down the beach towards the dock.

The two friends turned inland and walked closer to the small cliffs to their left. They hoped it would hide their approach. As they moved deeper in, they could see two additional ships behind the first one. With these three vessels added to the one they were chasing, that meant four Pirate ships. Without voicing their thoughts, both Albert and the Beast Master wondered if there were any more. Could there be a whole fleet?

"What do we do?" Albert asked, stopping behind a large rock at a bend in the beach.

"Not sure. We don't have a ship; we don't have a way to track them."

"Maybe we can sneak on and hide until they meet the other ship. They have to be connected, don't they? It just seems too coincidental."

"I would agree, but stowing away on a ship isn't an easy task. But there don't appear to be too many other options. Let's wait until dark, and then we will sneak through their defenses."

"How long until dark?"

The Beast Master looked at his watch. He adjusted the timepiece to the Martery Realm time cycle and pushed the small, black button to refresh the time. The digital screen forwarded ahead and read six in the evening. Pushing another button, he changed the mode and brought up a screen showing sunset and sunrise times. Comparing the times, he added the differences in his head and came up with a number.

"It looks like we have about two and a half hours. We should add another two hours to that to give them time to go to sleep."

"What are we going to do for four and a half hours?" Albert asked.

"Wait."

Four hours passed slowly. Albert and the Beast Master had ducked into a small cave and attempted to get some sleep, but neither could shut their eyes. They were too stressed about the task that was ahead of them. It came as a welcome release, when the alarm on the Minotaur's watch began to beep.

"It's time," the Beast Master said, rising off the soft sand and stretching his arms. "Let's go see if our friends are asleep."

Albert climbed to his feet and followed the yawning Minotaur out of the cave. The two companions made their way through the dark and stopped at the rock, from which they had viewed the Pirates earlier.

Small fires were spread sporadically across the beach with several Pirates lying near them. Albert transformed his eyes into those of a lion. The morph happened quickly and was hardly noticeable unless someone had stared into his blue eyes and watched them go deep-black.

"Let's see if any of them are awake." Albert said, scanning the beach with his enhanced eyesight. He watched each man for any movement and for the steadiness of his breathing.

"Is it clear?"

Albert scanned the rest of the campfires and

nodded agreement. The coast was clear, the Pirates were asleep, and they would have a chance to get aboard undetected. But they had to be careful.

"Everyone is asleep, including the guards at the docks. We should be safe."

The two friends stepped out from behind the rock and moved slowly across the center of the beach. The dark-black sky of an incoming storm provided perfect cover for Albert and the Beast Master. The only chance for them to be seen would be if someone awoke and saw the shadows cast by the low burning fires.

Within fifteen minutes, they had made it to the fringe of the Pirates' fires. The ragged bodies of the snoring men lay spread out across the sand at odd interlinking angles. There was going to be no avoiding the bodies. In several spots, they could see a tight fit that would force them to have to step over the criminals. It was going to be a lot harder than they originally had thought.

"We might as well get this over with," the Beast Master whispered, stepping forward.

Albert followed the Minotaur into the camp. The first couple of areas were easy. The men were far enough apart that the two friends were able to tiptoe through them without having to traverse an obstacle course of bodies. The fires in this part of the camp had almost burned down to white embers, and they found it easy to avoid the brightness of the flames.

The second area they passed into was quite a bit more tricky. Bodies of Pirates crisscrossed at every angle and forced the two companions to have to step over the snoring men.

Albert raised his leg and stretched his body over a sleeper. The huge man's wide body made it impossible for him to bring his second leg over. He was too spread out and found it difficult to keep his balance with one leg on each side of the giant Pirate. His body started to shake, and he was certain he was going to fall over and give away his location, but at the last minute, the large hand of the Minotaur reached down and lifted him out of the precarious situation.

"Thanks," Albert whispered.

The Beast Master acknowledged him with a nod and continued on through the camp.

The two friends developed a rhythm to get through the rest of the sleeping Pirates. The Beast Master would step across the snoring bodies with his wide stance and then reach over and lift his young companion to safety. They repeated this process over and over again until they made it to the dock area leading to the closest of the three ships.

The large dock was void of Pirates with the exception of one guard leaning against the side of the ship's hull near the plank. They couldn't see if the man was asleep, and the area was too dark for Albert to tell, even with his enhanced eyesight. With extreme care, the two friends stepped quietly down the dock, crouching-over, hoping to be less noticeable.

They were almost to the Pirate when they saw him turn towards them and stare directly at Albert and the Beast Master. In a sudden, yet fluid motion, the Pirate raised an odd-shaped gun from his side and pointed it at the two friends.

"Halt," the Pirate ordered.

Smiling, Albert and the Beast Master raised their hands and showed the Pirate that they were unarmed. They edged closer to the sentry and made a point to seem as scared as he wanted them to be.

"I said halt!" the Pirate yelled.

Albert looked back to the beach and saw a few Pirates stirring where they slept, but no one made a point to wake up and look for the source of the sound. They slowed their movement and drifted back to sleep next to their burned out fires.

"We did not mean to trespass," the Beast Master whispered. "We are lost and were hoping you could help us with directions."

"How did you get here? All of those men out there - surely one would have stopped you."

"No, no one did," Albert responded, innocently. "We just need to know ..."

"Silence," the Pirate interrupted. "Something is not right here. It would be best if I let the Captain work this out."

"I'm afraid I can't let you do that," the Beast Master said, stepping forward.

"What do you mean you ..."

The Beast Master rushed the Pirate and grabbed the wrist that held the gun. The Minotaur was twice as strong as the Pirate and was easily able to subdue him. With one punch to the head, the guard lost consciousness and dropped the pistol from his hand. As the Beast Master threw the Pirate into the water, he accidentally kicked the gun down the deck. It bounced a couple of times and landed at an angle on its trigger. A shot fired from it that echoed across the entire beach.

"Oh, no, they are waking up!" Albert exclaimed, watching men across the beach rise and look for the source of the gunshot.

"We have bigger problems," the Beast Master said, dropping to the ground on his butt. "I think I've been shot."

Albert turned towards his friend and could see a darkened circle of red forming in the center of the Minotaur's chest. The Beast Master held his hand over the wound, but the blood was flowing through his fingers.

"No! What do I do?" Albert asked, panic washing over him.

"You run."

"I'm not leaving you."

"You have to," the Beast Master said, coughing between each word. "I will only slow you down. You have to think about your Mother. You have to save her."

"But what about you?"

"I'll be fine. Trust me. I can get away."

"Then come with me."

"I will just slow you down. No, you go on. I will catch up to you later." The Minotaur smiled and nodded encouragingly to the young boy. "I promise."

"But …"

"No more but's. I have never lied to you before, and I won't start now. You and I will see each other again," the Beast Master said, his voice stern and cold. "Go. I will be fine."

Reluctantly, Albert stood and crawled into the ship. There was no one on board, and it was very easy to look for a hiding spot. The top deck would be too obvious a place to hide and, depending on the length of the journey, he could be easily discovered.

Albert made his way into the underbelly, hoping for a better hiding spot. He followed stairs down into the hold, up a hallway to a cabin of barrels and ducked down behind them. Outside, he could hear the Pirates approaching the ship. Albert hadn't felt this bad since the loss of his Grandparents. He couldn't believe he had to leave someone else to die. Uncontrollably, he started to cry.

CHAPTER TWENTY-THREE
DISCOVERY

Albert woke up behind the barrels and, at first, couldn't remember where he was. He stood up and looked around. The sound of Pirates, talking down the hall, shocked him back into reality and he dropped back down behind the barrier. He guessed his body just finally gave out and forced him into rest. He wasn't sure how long he had been asleep, nor did he even remember falling asleep.

Glad that he hadn't been discovered, Albert crawled out from behind the barrels and made his way down the hall. He listened carefully, making sure that the voices of the Pirates stayed far enough ahead of him to avoid detection. All he wanted was to be able to hear what they were talking about, and he was in luck. As he approached one corner, three Pirates were sitting at a table eating and talking about the events of the night.

"I still can't believe we couldn't find anyone," the tallest of the three Pirates said. "You would think that someone big enough to throw Dewy out in the water couldn't disappear that easy."

Albert smiled. The Beast Master had gotten away. He wasn't sure how and really didn't care. His friend was not captured. That was all that mattered.

"Maybe he used one of them there soda cans for transportation. I hear it's a weird feeling," a short, hairy Pirate added.

"It's no different than when our ship passes through one of them portals. How could it be? It's the same thing." The taller Pirate took a bite out of his bowl of beans after talking.

The third Pirate remained silent. He watched the two talk back and forth, not adding anything. Albert wondered if he was even capable of talking. Maybe he was a mute or something.

"Either way, the Captain is still angry we got no prisoners," the hairy Pirate said. "And I, for one, don't want to upset the Captain, especially with us hooking up with the Dutchman later. Captain Van Decken is as mean as they come."

"Yeah. I heard he be the one that captured the Princess."

"That's the *Queen,* you idiot," the third Pirate yelled, finally entering the conversation. "He captured the Queen of the Herionite Realm and I, for one, am worried about what will happen. This is a different world. Not like where we came from."

"You're crazy," the taller Pirate said. "We are Pirates. We rule the seas and, with the flying additions to our ships, the air as well. We are invincible. Aren't we?" He patted the hairy Pirate on the shoulder.

"Yep, invincible. And not to mention, we have lots of missiles if people get in our way."

The three Pirates sat in silence. Albert waited patiently for the conversation to continue, but was disappointed when they just continued to eat in still silence.

Albert could hear footsteps erupt from the down the hall. Someone was rushing his way. Quickly, he moved down the hall, trying the first door he came to. He slid into the room and gently shut the door behind him. Seconds later, the feet rushed past the door and into the room with the three Pirates.

"Captain Hilton has ordered all men on deck immediately," the Messenger said.

"Why?" the taller Pirate asked.

"We're about to come alongside the Dutchman, and Captain wants a proper crew for the hand off of the supplies."

The three Pirates responded quickly and rushed down the hall behind the messenger. When he was sure they were gone, Albert breathed a sign of relief and looked around the room he had stepped into.

"Wow," Albert said out loud, looking around the lavish surroundings.

Gold and jewels were spread across the tops of several tables. He wasn't sure if they were for decoration or for counting, but either way, they were beautiful. The bed and chairs were almost as fancy as the ones he remembered from his parents' castle ... almost. He figured that this must be the Captain's cabin.

The sound of rushing water banged against the large, two-pane window at the far end of the cabin. It caught Albert's attention and drew him away from the shiny objects to what was happening outside. Pulling back the drapes, he could see a fourth, larger ship pulling up alongside the one he had hidden on. He immediately recognized it as the one his Mother was on. It was the Dutchman.

The two ships pulled alongside each other, and large boards were placed between the decks of the two ships. Albert watched in awe, as men carrying large items began to cross over these flimsy-looking boards to the Dutchman. He figured it must be the supplies he had heard about. Not sure how long they would be loading, Albert frantically looked for a way to cross over.

The Dutchman was designed similar to the ship he was on. The back had a large window, which Albert guessed was the Captain's room, and various portholes and ropes hanging down the sides of the ship. The space between the two Pirate vessels was close to twenty feet. As a boy, he was sure he couldn't jump it. But as a lion, it would be a cinch.

Taking in a deep breath, Albert focused on his legs only. His feet, calves, and thighs began to expand and his shoes and pants were stretched to their limit. The sound of a small tear told Albert he had ripped something somewhere, but didn't care to look until he made the jump. He crouched down and pushed off hard with his lion's legs. His body flew through the air and landed safely on the small wood banister outside the window of the Dutchman's Captain's cabin.

Albert signaled his body to return to normal and quickly surveyed his clothes for the tear. His pants were fine, but his shoes had split where the rubber sole met the material; they were useless. He kicked them off his feet and into the water. As a general rule, he didn't like to litter, but he couldn't take the chance of someone finding them.

Reaching for the latch on the outside window, he pulled on the pane but found that it wouldn't open. He tugged again, but found the window was locked. There was no way in.

Above his head, Pirates passed back over the boards and pulled the wood planks back onto their ships. The transfer of supplies had been completed. From the angle of his position, Albert could see the two Pirate captains move to the edge of their respective boats and salute.

"Remember where we are meeting," Captain Van Decken called out.

"No problem. The other Captains and I will be ready for a fight," the stocky Captain Hilton replied.

"Good sailing."

"And to you," Captain Van Decken replied, disappearing from Albert's view.

Albert turned his attention back to the window. The curtains on the other side were wide open, and if the Captain entered his room, he would see Albert standing there. He had to get out of this area. If he couldn't go into the ship, maybe he could move about outside it.

Looking to his left and right, Albert located a rope a few feet away. Along the side of the ship, a rope hung about every three feet and would give Albert a way to make it to an old rope ladder hanging towards the other end of the ship.

He grabbed the closest rope and swung out along the ship. It was tougher than it had looked. As he hung by the rope, he could feel the strength in his arms start to dwindle and the material of the rope burn his hands. He wondered how long he could hang on? Then an idea struck him.

Albert focused on his upper arms, transforming them partially into a lion's. His human grip remained, but was augmented by the strength of the king of beasts. Not bothered by the ropes any longer, he swung out to the next line and the one after that. He moved from rope to rope gracefully until he found himself at the ladder. Letting the last rope go, he looked up to see if anyone had noticed his movement.

After a few moments of not attracting attention, he climbed up the ladder and stopped a few feet from the top banister, staying out of sight. He listened again for detection, and when nothing was heard, he moved up a little closer. Locking his arm around one of the top ladder rings, he signaled his arms to return to normal, and he waited. He wasn't sure what for, but he knew the sign would be there when it was time for him to act.

"I really want to go back to the desert now," Albert said to himself, looking at the water passing beneath his feet.

A bright flash appeared towards the front of the ship. Albert recognized it from earlier. The ship was heading into another portal. He wondered where they were headed now and if he would be okay hanging on the outside of the ship. Either way, he understood he didn't have a choice in the matter so he waited and watched to see what would happen.

The portal grew larger, and the front of the ship entered the light. He watched in awe, as piece by piece of the ship stretched and disappeared through the portal. It was almost upon him. Taking a deep breath, he gripped the ladder tighter and let the light engulf him. The taller Pirate had been right earlier; it felt the same as the can, but it didn't matter to Albert. He still loved the warm sensation that went along with portal transfers.

The Pirate ship disappeared into the portal, and the bright light dispersed behind them. A moment later the sea was calm and empty.

CHAPTER TWENTY-FOUR
THE FLYING DUTCHMAN

The Dutchman passed through the portal and settled back into the waters of the Amphibia Realm. From atop the ship's main deck, the Pirates moved from station to station checking and securing ropes and sails. Captain Van Decken stepped down from the upper level and motioned for Karter to join him.

"What can I do for you, Captain?" Karter asked, his voice eager to please.

"You have been with us for only a short time, but you have impressed me quite a bit," Captain Van Decken replied, putting his arm around the small boy.

"Some of the men, Kos included, would say you are trying too hard and that you are, more likely than not, a spy."

"A spy? That's crazy, Sir. I gave you Mason as a prisoner, I did ..."

"I said, *some men*. Not *me*. I happen to like your style. You remind me a lot of me when I was a boy, which is why I want you to come with me. I'm going to give you a chance my Father never did."

"What kind of chance, Sir?"

"I'm going to show you all of my secrets and treat you, not just like another Pirate, but like my own son. And we are going to start with the time device we have hooked up to our ship - the one we used to come twenty years ahead."

"Really!" Karter said, faking excitement. "That would be great."

"I know," the Pirate Captain said, sure of himself. "Come with me."

Captain Van Decken led Karter down through a hatch he had never seen before. It was dark and dry. Cobwebs hung from various corners, and the area appeared not frequently traveled. The Pirate led him down a corridor, down another flight of stairs and stopped at a room with a metal door, at the end of a short hall. The Pirate reached into his shirt and produced a key that hung on a chain around his neck. He unlocked the door and motioned for Karter to enter.

"Thank you, Sir."

Karter entered the room and wasn't impressed. Nothing stood out special in the room. The Captain made his way over to an old, beat up chest, sitting at an angle in the corner. He opened the lid to reveal a rectangular control device about the size of a shoebox. Lifting it up and paying careful attention not to pull on the cables flowing back into the chest, the Captain turned to Karter and lowered it for him to view.

"This is *so* cool," Karter said. "How does this thing work?"

"This dial here." Captain Van Decken pointed to the furthest left section. "It controls the amount of time to travel. The big marks with the numbers are years, and the twelve little marks in between are months. You control how far you will travel from your present time."

"How does it know to send you in the future or in

the past?"

"That would be this button over here. See, it says reverse and forward. That's it. Now, I am not clear on how it does what it does, or how Kos connected it to the ship, but it works like the portals. It opens one up wide and stays open for us and anything nearby to pass through."

"Like the other Pirate ships I saw at the supply rendezvous?"

"Yes. So, what do you think?"

"I am very impressed, sir. It's like a dream to be shown this," Karter lied. He wanted to hear about the Captain's other secrets, and if playing along got him there, then he would. "What other secrets do you want to show me, Sir?"

"Want to know how our ships fly?" the Captain asked. "How about the gold and items we have looted."

"Yes to both."

"Very well, we will stop by my cabin on the way to the upper deck. I will let you hold some of my gold medallions."

Karter smiled and watched the Captain gently put the device back down. He closed the lid to the chest and motioned for the boy to exit the room. After leaving, the Captain locked the door behind them and dropped the key back down his shirt on the string.

"After you, my boy," Captain Van Decken said, motioning for Karter to lead.

Karter was beginning to understand why the Captain was treating him so nice. In some weird way, the Pirate Captain was treating him like the son he never had. Boy, was this man in for a surprise!

CHAPTER TWENTY-FIVE
MASON'S FATE

Night came and went. Albert hung loosely from the rope ladder, his arms numb, but still keeping him secured. He was looking for a sign or a moment that would facilitate his rescuing his Mother. He had hoped that the Pirates would sleep at night as the others had on the beach. But this ship was run differently. There seemed to always be at least one or two men walking along the deck and making sure that everything was running smoothly. Albert hated efficiency.

The morning light was blinding, and it forced Albert to close his eyes. He wondered how much longer he could continue to hang, and he wanted more than anything to have a reason to jump on the ship and get this over with. He was tired and hungry. But he couldn't act too soon; he had to be careful. It was with this thought that a situation began to develop on the deck above him. His ears perked up and he forgot about his problems.

Captain Van Decken stepped toward the center of the ship and called out for all of his men to join him. Pirates poured out of every hatch and section of the ship and gathered around their leader.

"Good morning, men," Captain Van Decken said,

his chest puffed out. "Today I will let you partake in something that has been asked for over and over again. A plank walking."

"Who's going walk the plank?" an eager Pirate asked from the crowd.

"It appears that our captive, Mason, has outlived his usefulness. After last night's interrogation, I truly believe he knows nothing. He simply was unlucky that Karter sided with us instead. Karter, come up here and join me."

Karter pushed his way through the crowd and rushed to the Captain's side. He looked up at the proud Pirate and then to the two-headed bird sitting on his shoulder. The parrot squawked at him and then readjusted itself on its master's shoulder.

"This boy here has made today possible. We will show the Realm Regal and her precious Coalition that no matter who they send after us, we are not to be easily fooled and are *unstoppable*."

The Pirates started to cheer in unison. Albert peered over the edge of the banister and watched the crowd hoot and holler. How had Mason found the ship and come aboard? But more importantly, what had the Pirates done to him? This was the moment he would have to act. If not, Mason would be done for.

"Kos," the Captain called out.

"Aye, Sir," Kos said, stepping in front of the men and shooting dirty looks at Karter.

"Retrieve our guest from below and bring him here to me."

"Aye, aye, Sir." Kos disappeared into the crowd.

"You." The Captain pointed to a nearby man. "Get me a plank and push it out halfway from the port side. I want us to be ready to act."

"Aye, aye, Sir."

The Pirates went to work at locating the plank and moving it into position. A minute later, Kos and another Pirate dragged Mason on deck and threw him down to the ground at Captain Van Decker's feet. Behind them, another Pirate approached, nudging the beautiful Queen Nara to Mason's side. This was the first time Karter had seen her since he had come aboard. Her eyes pierced through him and caused him to lower his head. He couldn't handle her disapproving stare.

"I thought our cause would be better served if she watched the ordeal, Sir," Kos said, smiling and revealing his broken mouth of missing teeth.

"Good thinking, First Mate." The Captain turned to the Queen. "Now you will get to see what happens to those that challenge us."

"No!" Queen Nara screamed. "He has done nothing; spare him!"

Mason stood up and shook his head. "Don't waste your breath, Nara. He is beyond reason and knows nothing but cruelty."

"Take him," the Captain ordered.

Nara clung to Mason and put her arms around him. Kos pulled on her and separated the two captives. Mason didn't bother to fight.

"It will be all right," Mason said, nodding to Queen Nara.

"I love you," Nara said. "I always have, and I am sorry we lost so much time."

"No apologies," Mason replied, smiling. "For the record, I love you too."

Nara saw Karter standing next to the Pirate and asked, "Why, Karter? He took you in; he gave you a home. How could you?"

"It's complicated, Mom. Maybe if you and Dad had been better parents, I wouldn't be like this." It hurt Karter to see the reaction on his Mother's face. Tears began to flow down her cheeks and the guilt of many years flowed across her expression.

"Better parents?"

"Yeah, I told the Captain how you and Father would beat me every birthday and never gave me a cake. I even told him about your killing my dog and hanging me in the dungeon when I disagreed with you."

"But we didn't ..." Nara stopped herself. Something wasn't right. Karter had told the Captain the false stories for a reason. She thought back to Mason's comment about how it might have something to do with a plan Albert had come up with, and she didn't want to blow her son's story and put him in jeopardy as well. Instead she just ignored the comments.

"Everything that has happened to you was deserved."

"Enough of this," Captain Van Decken yelled. "Move him onto the plank."

Clapping with excitement, the Pirates pushed Mason out on the two-foot wide board. They poked at him with their swords and forced him out over the water. He looked down at the large waves crashing against the Dutchman's wooden hull.

Albert couldn't wait any longer. He climbed over the railing and landed on the deck with a loud thud. The crew was so noisy and excited they didn't notice him come up behind them.

"Hey," Albert yelled, displeased with them not hearing him. He hoped for the dramatic entrance like he had seen in the movies. He wanted all the Pirates to turn to him and marvel at how he got there. "Please stop that."

The Pirates twisted towards him and stared in confusion. With all the men in the way, the Captain couldn't see Albert, the child, screaming out in the back, so he motioned for the men to separate. When they did, he saw the scrawny form of Albert.

"And who might you be, young man?" the Pirate Captain asked.

"My name is Albert, and I am here for my family and friends."

"Albert," Captain Van Decken said, stroking the tip of the beard on his chin. "I have heard a lot about you. Tell me. How is it that you seemed to locate us in the middle of the sea?"

Albert smiled. Finally, the question was asked. Unfortunately, he had forgotten his snappy response. Instead, he just grinned and put his hands on his hips and pushed his chest out.

"There isn't anything that I can't do. Now, about my Mother's and Mason's release. It's time for us all to leave."

"You think that you can do something against all my men? Ah, that's right. You're a full transformer aren't you?"

Albert nodded in agreement.

"You may be a full transformer." The Captain smiled. "But that won't do you much good against swords. But perhaps we can work something out to avoid any unnecessary violence. First, say hello to my little friend, our mascot."

The Captain took the two-headed parrot off his shoulder and held him out at arm's length. The bird flew off of his shoulder and crossed the distance to Albert. Flapping its wings continuously, the bird floated in front of Albert's head.

"Albert, look out," Mason yelled, from the end of the plank. But it was too late; the bird had already started to hypnotize Albert.

"You be quiet," a Pirate yelled at Mason, forcing him further out on the plank.

The feeling passing over Albert was like nothing he had ever felt. His legs felt as flimsy as jelly, and he found it took all of his energy to keep them straight. Standing was becoming increasingly difficult. Thoughts of his Mother and Mason drifted away. He didn't seem to care about anything around him.

His mind drifted back to his life before his transformation. He was sitting at a table eating his breakfast with his Grandpa and Grandma. They were smiling and staring at him. At first Albert thought all of his adventures and experiences had been a dream, but then the image of the two-headed bird appeared over the table - its swirling eyes staring deeply into his own, making him not care about anything. But he had to care; there were people to rescue.

Suddenly, he found himself back on the Pirate ship. The image of his Grandparents faded as quickly as it had come. In his mind, he hungered to go back, but he knew it wouldn't happen. It had only been a dream.

His mind pushed the trance image out, and he tried to focus on his current situation. He couldn't move, but Albert knew where he was. And in front of him floated the odd bird. He could faintly hear Mason calling out to him, but wasn't clear on what his guardian was saying.

The bird moved in closer to Albert and forced his lips open with its bony claws. Small drops of blood dripped down the corners of his mouth and the bird's feet tore at his skin. The bird pushed its beak into Albert's mouth and opened it wide.

CHAPTER TWENTY-SIX
KARTER'S SURPRISE

Albert watched helplessly as the two-headed bird paused, swallowed and prepared to spit its beast inhibiting venom into his mouth. He didn't know exactly what would happen, but he was sure that the bird was going to do something to him that he wouldn't like. He could feel the bird slip its beak deeper into his mouth. Whatever was going to happen would happen soon.

Suddenly, his situation changed. One moment the bird was in front of him, then he heard a loud squawk and the bird was gone. All that remained was a puff of feathers that gently floated its way down to the ground ... Albert shook the daze away and focused on what happened. Karter was just bringing back his fist, feathers sticking between his fingers.

"Home run!" Karter said, a smile on his face.

The crew erupted in shouts of shock and surprise, but none was as surprised as Captain Van Decken. He was stunned and dismayed. Karter had punched the bird before it could deliver the poison to the full transformer. Albert was free, and Karter had betrayed the Captain.

"Everything going according to our plan?" Albert

asked, now fully awake.

"No problem, Bro. Everything is set, and we are ready to get out of here."

"Even the ..."

"I disabled the portal jumper and set their time jumper in the method I told you in the bottle. You did get the bottle?"

"Yep."

Mason smiled from the end of the plank. He knew that Karter couldn't have turned evil, but his happiness was small compared to that of Nara, who immediately sprang to her boy's side. She pushed her way through the Pirates and touched each boy on the shoulder as she turned to face the angry crew.

"What! That's not possible," the Pirate Captain exclaimed in rage. He and the crew stared blankly at the family, dazed.

"Not at all," Karter responded. "Last night when you fell asleep, I simply sneaked in and removed the key from around your neck. Simple."

"Get them," Captain Van Decken ordered, turning red with anger.

"It's showtime," Karter said, stepping back from Albert.

Albert arched his head back and dropped to the ground on his hands and knees. His skin bubbled and stretched away from his bones as it grew and reshaped itself. The clothes on his back ripped and fell to the side as his growing body could no longer be contained with in them. The paws of a lion were noticeable first on the bubbling body; then Albert's head enlarged and grew the golden hair of a lion's mane. The whole frame of his body took on a new structure. Where Albert had been, now stood a lion, four times the size of the young boy.

The Pirate crew stepped back and watched with large, wide eyes as the young Prince's body morphed into a lion. They had never seen a full transformer actually change before, and it frightened them beyond words. Standing frozen with fear and not able to move, they watched in amazement until the full transformation was completed. Not knowing what to do, they quietly waited for what would happen next.

"What are you doing?" the Pirate Captain yelled, not taken in with the wondrous transformation of the boy. "Get him."

The Pirates rushed towards Albert, the Lion, and the corner of his lips rose in the closest thing to a smile the beast could form. He jumped forward and knocked down four Pirates with the weight of his body. Two others backed away from him and tumbled over the edge of the ship into the water.

Nara didn't wait for her son to finish the men; she ran into the Pirates jumping and performing a roundhouse kick. As her body spun around, the side of her foot connected with the closest Pirate. He dropped to the ground in pain, but she didn't wait for him to get back up. She dropped her fist into his chest and incapacitated him.

Karter knew his strengths and limits. He wouldn't make much of a difference in a fight, but he could help save Mason. Rushing across the deck, he dove at the knees of the Pirate holding Mason at bay with his sword. The scruffy looking Pirate fell forward, bounced on the plank and fell off into the water. The wood began to shake and Mason lost his balance, and toppled from the wood plank.

Mason landed in the water with a splash big enough to blind the Pirate that landed there a few seconds before him. The Pirate jumped onto Mason's head and tried to push him under the ocean.

Remembering that Mason couldn't transform into his beast face, Karter looked around the deck for something to throw. A few feet away he spotted a brick, something the Pirates used to keep rope from blowing loosely in the wind. He walked over and reached down to pick it up. As his hand gripped the brick, a boot stepped across his fingers and pushed down. In extreme pain, Karter looked up and saw the scowling face of the Pirate Captain.

"You think you are so smart," Captain Van Decken said, anger in his voice. "You may have fooled me for a little while, but it won't take long to fix whatever damage you did. And then I will make you walk the plank with the rest of your family."

"I don't think so," Queen Nara called out. She launched herself into the air, and her boot collided with the right cheek of the angry Pirate Captain. "Go help Mason."

Karter smiled back to his Mom as he picked up the brick and rushed to the side. Mason was struggling with the Pirate in the water, but his swimming skills were not as good as the Pirate's, and it was apparent that he was losing.

"Duck!" Karter yelled down.

Mason sank underwater, and Karter threw the brick with all of his might. The red projectile flew through the air and hit the Pirate straight on the forehead. The man stopped moving as he instantly dropped unconscious. Mason surfaced on the water and waved up to Karter.

"Thank you."

"Glad I could help," Karter replied, throwing a rope down to him.

Karter stepped to the side, just as a large, heavy-set Pirate slid across the deck colliding with the banister. He looked up and saw his brother, the Lion, jumping and swiping to the left and right.

"Hey, that one almost hit me," Karter yelled, humor in his voice.

Albert, the Lion, nodded in agreement, and Karter thought for sure his brother had learned to make his lion face smile.

Karter knew that Albert would have been able to finish the fight quickly if he had used his claws. One of the first lessons they had taught him at the Beast School was *not* to use your gift to kill. There was something wrong with using the balance of nature to become a predator. They taught him to use it for protection and to better the community, but never to kill anyone. Because of this, in which he believed wholeheartedly, he swiped at his attackers with full force, but no claws. They would fly or drop away, but soon came back with the same ferocity. His brother was not ending the battle.

"We have to get out of here," Albert, the Lion, called out. "I can fight all day, but we need to get Mom to safety."

"The boat's ready," Karter replied. Meet me in the aft section."

"The what?" Albert, the Lion, asked, ducking a swing of a sword.

"Sorry, that's sailor talk. I mean the back of the boat." Karter scurried towards the back of the Pirate ship, where he had prepared a small rowboat to drop into the water.

Mason had made it up to the deck and heard the exchange between Karter and Albert. He looked around for Nara and was happy when he saw her among the Pirates, fighting back with the talent she had spent so long perfecting. A kick here, a kick there, and Pirates fell like toy soldiers.

"We need to go, Nara," Mason called out, heading towards the back.

"On my way," the Queen replied, performing a circle kick and sending another low-life sailing over the edge of the ship.

Albert, the Lion, watched each of his family make their way to the back. It was time for him to join them. He roared with all of his might, scaring the sailors closest to him. The Pirates staggered back, leaving an open path for him to the lifeboat. Quickly, he ran down the deck and met his family by the boat. They had all climbed into it and were slowly lowering themselves into the water.

"You have to change," Mason said, looking up at Albert, the Lion. "You are too heavy and too big to ride in here with us."

"But my clothes ripped, I don't have anything to wear."

"It isn't anything we haven't seen before," Queen Nara said, motioning him to join them.

Reluctantly, Albert transformed into his naked human form and jumped into the boat. Karter was giggling and didn't try to hide it.

"Stop it, Karter!" Albert screamed, reaching out to grab him.

Nara put her arms between the boys and separated them. "No fighting, boys." Nara smiled with that statement; it made her feel like a Mother.

"Take this," Mason said, throwing Albert his oversized shirt.

Nara looked at the hairy, blue chest of her ex-husband and smiled. She had forgotten how great a shape he was in and although she would never admit it, she liked him better without his shirt.

"Thanks," Albert replied, slipping the shirt over his body.

Karter still chuckled.

"Shut up!" Albert screamed.

The small boat sank into the water and floated safely next to the Pirate ship. Mason activated the small motor on its back, and the tiny vessel sailed away from the Pirate ship. The Dutchman didn't pursue them.

"I disabled their steering mechanisms," Karter said, dropping a few metal screws into the hand of Mason. "It was pretty easy."

"All part of the plan," Albert said, proudly. "All part of the plan."

"You should have told me about your plan," Mason scolded. "I could have seriously hurt Karter if I had tried to escape. Did you think about that or was this plan just reckless?"

"You were already gone. I didn't have very much choice, did I?"

Mason didn't reply. He knew that Albert was right. He steered the ship towards the Northern

Province. From there, they could head home.

"What's that?" Albert asked, pointing at three bright lights that started to quickly expand.

"Those are ship portals," Karter commented. "And there's three of them. They must belong to the other Pirate ships."

The three light circles opened wide and the Pirate ships sailed into the Amphibia Realm. Moments later, the portals closed behind them and the four escapees found themselves surrounded by Pirates.

"There wouldn't be any chance, would there, that you had disabled those as well?" Albert asked. "Because that would be really helpful right about now."

Karter stared at his brother and shook his head, *no*. He turned to Mason and looked for an answer to their new dilemma.

"Don't look at me," Mason said. "You did the rescuing."

Mason turned the tiny ship and started heading back towards the Dutchman. He hoped to pass along the other side and travel a different direction, but the three Pirate ships were too quick. They angled themselves towards the tiny boat and boxed them in. There was nowhere for Mason to take the boat. They were trapped, and that meant they would probably see Captain Van Decken again.

CHAPTER TWENTY-SEVEN
AGAINST THE RIFT

"So, since we have some time before we are captured," Mason said, watching the Pirate ships close in around them. "How did you disable their time and portal devices?"

"It was pretty easy," Karter replied, excited. "Both devices were no bigger than a loaf of bread, and they kept them in these isolated rooms. After I stole the key from the Captain, I just went in, pulled them out of their holders and threw them overboard."

"You threw a time traveling device overboard?" Albert asked. "Don't you know how cool it would have been to play with that?"

"What was I supposed to do? Your plan wasn't big on the details."

"Don't make me come over there and smack you," Albert replied. "Because I will do it."

"Stop fighting, boys," Nara chimed in, again happy to be the Mother.

Beep! Beep! Beep!

"What's that?" Albert asked, looking at Mason's chiming boot.

"It's my tracking device," he replied, digging the pen-looking mechanism out of its hiding place.

172

"Why is it beeping?" Nara asked.

"I'm not sure."

"Look!" Karter screamed, pointing beyond the Pirate ships surrounding them. Several large portals began to form in the distance. He counted ten in all. Turning back to Albert he shook his head in confusion. He had only known of four Pirate ships. *Where were the other ones coming from?*

"I thought there were only four Pirate ships," Karter said. "Really! That's all the Captain talked about. But from those portals, it appears there are at least ten more coming here."

"No one blames you," Albert said, thoughtfully. "It just means we need to work a little harder to escape this time. And just in case you were wondering, I wish we were back in the desert."

The pen device in Mason's hand stopped beeping, and a voice came across the microphone.

"This is Admiral Nakita. We are aware of your situation and ask that you duck while we get the Pirates' attention."

Large, shiny, silver ships boomed out of the ten portals. The insignia of the Realm Regal was displayed largely across their sides. It wasn't more Pirate ships at all; it was a Coalition rescue.

"It's the Coalition!" Albert exclaimed. "We are saved."

The large, metal ships completely passed through the portals, and instantly multiple missiles shot from the guns on their decks. Albert followed one projectile over their heads and watched it collide with the front of the Dutchman. It obliterated the wood from the Pirate ship and left a large hole. The ship lunged forward and started to sink.

Missiles flew off the other nine ships and collided with the other Pirate vessels causing similar damage. In a matter of seconds the threats from the sea terrorists had been ended.

"That should do it," Mason commented, turning the tiny ship towards the lead Coalition vessel.

"What happens next?" Albert asked. "Do they execute them or something?"

"This isn't your Father's land, Albert. The Coalition only shoots to disable. The Navy should dispatch troops next, to rescue the Pirates and take them into custody for trial. You will learn to understand that we have moved beyond killing, just to kill. We are more civilized and curb our fighting."

"Then, what's that?" Karter asked, pointing to several more missiles erupting into the air from the Coalition vessels.

The missiles flew over their heads and collided sporadically across the hulls of the Pirate ships. The wood splintered and shattered across the open sea. The sounds of the blasts could be heard miles away. The echo was deafening.

"Stop!" Mason yelled, standing and waving his arms wide. "They are disabled. What do you think you are doing? Stop Firing!"

CHAPTER TWENTY-EIGHT
THE ATTACK

Admiral Nakita stared proudly at the view screen in front of him. Their precision shots had disabled the ships as planned. He walked over to his gunner and put his hand on the young man's shoulder.

"Signal all ships to stop firing. Dispatch the troops and rescue teams. We will house the prisoners on our vessel."

"No," a soft, feminine voice called from the doorway of the ship's bridge.

Admiral Nakita spun on his heels and was shocked to see the Realm Regal standing behind him, countermanding his order. He stared blankly at her.

"I want you and all our ships to keep firing," the Realm Regal ordered.

"But Regal," Admiral Nakita argued. "They are disabled; we have won."

"No one will win until they are completely destroyed. They killed my Mother twenty years ago. I will not give them another chance. Now continue to fire, or I will relieve you of your duty."

The Realm Regal stepped into the room and the corners of her beautiful mouth turned down in a scowl. She stared at the Admiral waiting for his response. It was clear she would not take *no* for an answer.

Admiral Nakita thought about the threat. He knew it was wrong, but with only a year left until his retirement, he didn't want to do anything to jeopardize the pension he would receive. He turned back to the gunner and took his order back.

"The Realm Regal has given us a direct order, gunner. Signal all our ships to continue firing at the terrorists. We want nothing left."

"You can't!" Lisa yelled, running around the Regal and onto the bridge. "It isn't right, no matter what they have done."

"Is there someone selling tickets outside the bridge door?" Admiral Nakita said, frustrated. "This is supposed to be a secured area. You need to leave the bridge immediately, young lady."

"They may be terrorists, but they don't deserve to be slaughtered. You have won; they are disabled, and we should capture them. Tell them, Regal."

"I will not be lectured by a child," the Realm Regal said, not turning to look at Lisa. "We are happy that you escaped from King John and thankful that you came right to us for help. The information you provided was invaluable. But I will not have you talk to me in that manner. I lead; you follow."

"I used to think you were smart. But this is just desperate."

"Admiral, remove her from the bridge," the Realm Regal ordered. "It is obvious that she will not leave on her own."

"With all due respect, she is right, Regal. This is not the right move to …"

"Enough!" the Realm Regal interrupted. "You

will do as I ask, or I will relieve you of your command. I will *not* have you fighting me on this. Is that fully understood?"

Admiral Nakita nodded in acknowledgement and motioned for a sentry in the corner to remove the small girl from the room.

"Wait," Lisa yelled, dodging the first attempt from the guard to grab her. "Regal, what's wrong with you? You're supposed to set the example. It's not right just to wipe out people that have done wrong. Aren't we supposed to try to change them?"

"I still hear her talking," the Realm Regal said, her tone bordering on anger. "I thought I asked for her to be removed."

The sentry rushed up to Lisa and pulled her from the room. Lisa fought to stay on the bridge, but the large guard overpowered her. She hated being so young and small. Lately, grownups seemed to be using that against her.

Mason sat down in the rowboat, convinced that no one would listen to him. He watched in silence as missile after missile sped through the sky and collided with Pirate ships. The remaining parts of the ships, quickly sank beneath the surface of the water. There wasn't much left to destroy, but the bombardment continued at a terrifying rate.

The Dutchman was the first Pirate ship to sink. Mason could see the pain-stricken face of Captain Van Decken, as the last part of the ship he was standing on sank into the water. The ship was gone. Seconds later, a few heads broke the surface of the water.

Mason could see at least nine Pirates, including the Captain, treading water and awaiting their capture.

Mason was happy to see some survivors, but that all changed when he heard the launch of another missile and watched it fly over their heads. It struck the water where the Pirates had been floating and exploded in a bright flash, causing water and ship debris to scatter. As the smoke and water cleared, Mason studied the water carefully. The Pirates were no longer on the surface. He was sure the missile had ended their lives.

Frustrated and full of anger, Mason fingered the accelerator on the tiny ship's motor and sped to the lead ship. He needed to understand what was going on and why they had become barbarians. Those Pirates had been helpless in the water; they didn't deserve to have their lives ended that way. Life in general was too precious just to be thrown away.

The small vessel carrying Mason, Nara and the boys pulled up along side the lead ship. A large door slid open, and a metal platform extended to their boat. Three Coalition sailors stepped out on the platform and helped Albert and Karter out of the boat. They extended their hand to Nara, who shook it off and climbed out on her own. Next, Mason moved onto the platform and kicked the boat away from the larger vessel.

"Is the Admiral on board?" Mason asked, his voice angry.

"Yes, Sir," the closest sailor answered. "He and the Realm Regal are both here."

"Where are they?"

"They are on the bridge, but …"

"Thank you," Mason coldly said, storming off into the ship.

"Wait!" Nara called out, running after Mason. "Don't do anything stupid."

"This is going to be good," Karter said, as he and Albert followed the two adults.

CHAPTER TWENTY-NINE
UN-HAPPILY EVER AFTER

Mason, storming up the hall, found his anger diffuse slightly when he saw Lisa standing outside the bridge door. She noticed him, and they hugged.

"I tried to stop them, Dad, but they wouldn't listen," Lisa said. "The Realm Regal isn't thinking straight. She had me thrown out for disagreeing with her. She ordered them to keep firing. Something about revenge for her Mother."

"I know, Honey," Mason said, rubbing her head. "Let's get to the bottom of this."

Mason opened the door and stepped into the bridge. Lisa was about to follow when she noticed Nara, Karter and Albert rushing down the hallway. She wanted to call out to her Mother and tell her everything, but as promised, held that emotion in check. She smiled and greeted the Queen, who smiled back and rushed in after Mason.

"You're okay!" Albert exclaimed, reaching out and hugging Lisa.

"I managed to escape. It wasn't easy, but the tunnels you described helped. And you were so right; it is fun to frustrate Flug."

"Hey, guys, catch me up here. Lisa was with

Flug?" Karter asked. "When did that happen?"

"Where did you go?" Lisa asked.

"We can talk about this later," Albert said. "But for the highlights: Karter, Dad captured Lisa when I went to find the trace on Mom. And Lisa - Karter and I faked our fight so he could go undercover. Now that it's all out, let's go back up Mason."

Albert ducked onto the bridge. Lisa and Karter stared at each other in silence. They had both been through a lot recently. They made a silent pact to discuss it later, but didn't want to miss the argument.

"I bet he wishes he was back in the desert," Lisa said, smiling.

Karter nodded in agreement as they ducked into the bridge after Albert.

"Why? Just tell me that," Mason screamed, his hands on his hips.

"They were a threat," the Realm Regal said. "And I don't appreciate your questioning me. I did what I felt was necessary. And frankly, I don't see why you are so upset; we won. The victory is ours and the Realm Pirates will not bother us again."

"There are no winners or victors in war, only survivors. I thought we had progressed far enough to understand that. We aren't savages. We don't have the right to kill people just because we don't think they can be rehabilitated. This makes us no better than King John, the Dark Red." Mason turned back to the boys. "No offense."

"None taken," Albert replied.

"Those men were helpless; we could have captured them."

"That is quite enough, Mason!" the Realm Regal

yelled back.

The crew on the bridge shifted in their seats, uncomfortable with the exchange. Admiral Nakita stepped to the side of Mason and watched as the Realm Regal squirmed in anger.

"What has happened to us?" Mason asked. "We are supposed to be evolved."

"They were terrorists!" the Realm Regal shouted. "Everyone seems to forget this. They took from us, they killed our people. I just returned the favor. An eye for an eye. You know as well as I that these men would not have been rehabilitated. They would have schemed and plotted a way to escape. In the end, we would have had to execute them anyway."

"We have laws preventing capital punishment."

"Maybe I should change that, as well."

Mason shook his head in frustration. He knew what he had to do, but just couldn't believe it had come to this. The Realm Regal had anger and savageness in her eyes. She was serious about trying to get the death penalty reinstated. What was to become of their society with a leader believing that death without condition was alright?

"Furthermore," the Realm Regal continued. "You are quite lucky that I don't dismiss you for this insubordination and for disobeying my direct orders and going after your sweetheart."

"You would dismiss a member of your cabinet that has served the Coalition well for so many years because he disagrees with you?" Mason asked. "Does that honestly sound right to you?"

The Realm Regal continued to stare at Mason, not saying a word. She crossed her arms and didn't make any attempt to deny it.

"Then I guess I have no other choice," Mason continued. "My tracer led you to these Pirates, and so, in a way, this is all my fault. I thought you were better than this. But my hands are tied. Since you have become this way, I do not want to be associated with the Coalition anymore."

"What are you saying?" the Realm Regal asked, uncrossing her arms.

"I am saying, I quit."

"No," Lisa said, stepping in front of her Father. "You can't quit; we have done so much good. We can help so many ..."

"No, I must." Mason said, putting his hands on Lisa's shoulders. "It's the right thing to do. Effective immediately, I resign."

"Mom, say something to him; he can't do this. Not now." Lisa turned towards Nara and motioned for her to help.

Nara and Mason exchanged looks of confusion. They shook their heads at each other confirming that neither had told the rambunctious girl the truth. How had Lisa discovered that Nara was her Mother? The two parents came to the realization at the same time and turned to Albert and Karter.

"Hey, don't look at me," Albert said, pointing at Karter. "I'm not the big mouth Herionite around here."

"It was an accident," Karter replied, a slight smile of apology on his face. "It just slipped out. I tried to deny it but she is too smart. She saw right through me."

"Well, that about covers that secret. It's fine now. But Lisa, I'm sorry, your Father is right. And as far as him quitting, that goes for me, too," Queen

Prince Albert, Book 3: The Realm Pirates

Nara said from behind. "I can no longer stay with King John. I have provided you years of service at no gain to myself. Finding you no better than him, there is no reason for me to continue. Effective immediately, I am resigning as well. You can find someone else to spy."

The look on the Realm Regal's face was one of shock and confusion. She truly did not believe she had done anything wrong. But having two of her top operatives quit would be hard to recover from. She would figure it out though, she didn't need them. They were only two people, after all.

"Fine," the Realm Regal said. "Then, as civilians, you are in an unauthorized area. Sentry, please escort these people to a public area."

"Yes, Ma'am," the sentry replied, ushering the five people out of the room.

The door shut behind them, and the Realm Regal turned to the wall. She wanted to make sure no one could see her face. Tears rolled down her cheeks as she wondered where to go from here. Had she crossed the line? Had she led her people down a path that was to the past, not to the future? What would she do now? Her men and her agents had corrected her, and deep down she knew they were right. But she just couldn't let the Pirates live. They would have come after her, just like they did her Mother.

"Regal," Admiral Nakita said. "Captain Antilles reports there are no survivors, and we are ready to get our vessels under way."

"Good," the Realm Regal replied, wiping the tears from her cheeks. "Set course for the Capital. It's time we head home.

CHAPTER THIRTY
RESOLUTIONS

Mason and Nara sat at the kitchen table holding hands and looking into each other's eyes. They were extremely happy about their announcements and slightly nervous about how the children would react when they heard them. Mason looked at his watch and held up two fingers to the beautiful woman. The kids would be home soon from their errands.

Albert was the first to return. He came in from the front door and looked around for Mason and his Mother. He knew they were here. They had made it very clear he had to be back by eleven.

"Mason. Mom," Albert called out, dropping his backpack on the couch.

"In the kitchen," Nara replied.

Albert entered the kitchen and sat down at the table. He scooted his chair up next to his Mother and asked, "So, what's up?"

"Let's wait for Karter and Lisa," Mason said. "How is the Beast Master?"

"For such a big thing, he really is a baby," Albert said, smiling. "You wouldn't believe how much he is still complaining. They finally released him from the hospital today, and when I got him home, all he could talk about was the food in the hospital."

"Did he tell you how he got off the dock and escaped the Pirates?"

"Oh, my gosh, like a hundred times. And I am sure he will be talking about it for weeks, even months. He is very proud of it."

"So what was the story?" Nara asked.

"I don't remember all of his big details, but basically, he said he rolled off into the water just after I boarded the ship. According to him, he made his way across the wood to the edge of the dock before the Pirates could get to the plank. He rolled into the water, which was below freezing temperature, if you believe him, and he waited in pain for the ships to leave the area."

"But if the temperature were below freezing, then the water would have been solid ice, not flowing water," Mason added.

"I tried to tell him that, but you know him. Won't listen and insists he is right. But anyway, after the ships were gone, he crawled back onto the beach and walked for three miles until he reached a civilized area, and then the people of the Dooter Province helped him get to a hospital."

"Three miles with a gun shot?" Nara questioned. "That seems like a lot. And isn't the Dooter Province just half a mile from the docks?"

"Again, he insisted it was three miles. I didn't try to fight with him. I was just glad he was okay. It was a relief."

The three people heard the front door open and, from the stomping of the feet, knew it must be Karter. He shut the door behind him and called out for his brother and Mother.

"We're in here," Mason said.

Karter joined them in the kitchen a few moments later and took a seat at the table.

"So, what's up?" Karter asked.

"Let's wait for Lisa," Nara replied. "She should be here soon. How did the delivery of the message go? Any problems?"

"Not at all, Mom. I took it to the messenger service in town, and they said that Dad would have it in a few days or so."

The front door opened and Lisa made her way to the kitchen. She took a seat at the table and looked toward Mason and Nara.

"So, now that we are all here," Mason said. "We have information to share with you. We are very happy about it and hope you will be as well."

The children all leaned forward in anticipation. They were more than eager to hear it.

"Your Mother and I have decided to get married again." Mason scanned the faces of the children and waited for the news to sink in.

Albert, Karter and Lisa all smiled in hearty agreement. They looked at each other, their eyes dancing with happiness and approval.

"And if it's okay with you boys," Nara added. "Mason has asked to adopt you two - to move from being your guardian to becoming your step-Father."

"That would be great," Albert burst out, unable to contain his excitement.

"Karter?" Mason asked. "How about you? Are you okay with this?"

Karter stood up, walked over to Mason and

hugged him tightly, as tears of joy rolled down his cheeks. He hadn't remembered being this happy. Mason returned the hug with a smile.

"Of course, I am okay with this," Karter said, releasing his grip.

"We have one more piece of news," Mason said. "It's just as big."

"More?" Lisa replied. "What more could you have to say?"

"Now that we have quit the Coalition your Mother and I asked ourselves what should we do now. I talked to the Headmaster, and we have both been offered positions at the Braunite Beast School."

"You're going to be teachers!" Lisa exclaimed, sarcastically. "Heaven help me. Next year is going to be a nightmare."

EPILOGUE
KING JOHN'S BAD NEWS

King John, the Dark Red, sat quietly in the darkness of his bedchambers. He had heard that the Pirates had been destroyed and his wife rescued. But where was she? Shouldn't she have returned? Shouldn't she be here with him?

He had to admit that he was happy that he did not have to pay the ransom. The money was back in his safe, and once again he felt safe. He tried to tell himself that the money was not more important than his wife, but he just wasn't sure. Hearing that she had been rescued had definitely made him happy, but keeping his money had as well.

Knock! Knock! Knock!

A knock at the door broke the King out of his depression. He crossed to the door and jerked it open wide.

"What is it?" King John asked.

A shaking, young guard jutted out to the King a red envelope.

"This came for you, Your Majesty," the nervous guard said.

King John took the envelope, and slammed the door in the guard's face. He could hear the man exclaim in pain as the door collided with the soldier's open hand. It brought a slight smile to his face. The King tore open the envelope and pulled out the letter inside. He immediately recognized the writing as Nara's.

"Dear John," the King read out loud. "I am writing to tell you that I *will not* be returning to your castle. I have decided to raise our boys and finally live in happiness. I will raise them to take the kingdom from you someday. You can be sure of that. I am not sure how many years it will take, but eventually they will return to overthrow you."

King John swallowed hard. The stinging words of his Queen cut him deep inside. He couldn't believe what he was reading.

"You need to know that I never wanted to be there with you," the King read on. "I worked for the Coalition the whole time, and passed them your secrets. They have the information about all your planned attacks and skirmishes for the next year. I would suggest that you cancel any strategies you have and make a strong attempt to go straight. They will be watching you. Don't attempt to find me. Goodbye, and good luck."

King John crumpled the letter in his hand. He rolled it into a ball and threw it across the room. Anger flowed through his blood and drove him to kick over the chair closest to him.

"Ahhhggg!!!" King John screamed in anger. "I can't believe this!"

Across the room, he saw the picture of Albert and Karter that the Queen had kept on her nightstand. He crossed the room and picked it up. Pulling back his hand, he punched the glass once and then a second time. The glass of the frame scattered and fell to the floor. The King tossed the remaining frame across the room. It shattered against the bedroom wall.

The door to the King's bedchamber flew open and Flug rushed in. His sword was drawn and he looked anxiously about the room, Seeing there was no immediate danger, he turned to the monarch. "Is everything all right, Your Majesty?" Flug asked, concern in his voice. "The guards said they heard you scream."

"Everything is *not* okay," King John replied. "We have something to take care of."

The King crossed the room and picked up the shattered picture of Albert and Karter. Brushing away the pieces of glass, he held it up and showed it to the Captain of his Guards.

"These two." King John pointed at the boys. "Somehow, they turned their Mother against me and they need to pay for that."

"The Queen is against you?"

"She will not be returning. But that won't stop us. We have to come up with a plan to get her back and end the lives of these two boys."

"Yes, Your Majesty," Flug replied. "We can definitely do that.

PRINCE ALBERT WILL RETURN IN,
PRINCE ALBERT, BOOK FOUR:
THE LOST REALM,
HIS FOURTH ADVENTURE
ON THE ROAD TO BE KING.

Brian Daffern started writing and telling stories in high school to entertain family and friends. A chance meeting with the famous writer, Raymond Feist, encouraged him to pursue his dream. After winning several writing contests and short story awards, Brian turned his attention to novels.

He works as a computer specialist and lives with his wife and four lovely daughters in Northern California. Inspired by the imagination and innocence of his children, Brian has created several worlds of imagination including this book, his third in the *Prince Albert Series*. Brian's imagination seems endless, so look for as many more book as you the readers continue to enjoy. Brian hopes to teach children the value of life and of love through his adventure and fantasy novels.

Look for his first book, *Prince Albert in a Can,* which is followed by *Prince Albert, Book Two: The Beast School.* Both may be found at our website, www.hickorytales.com or at bookstores and online bookstore sites.